T0118400

Friends,Colleagues and Bastards

Stuart Bell

authorHOUSE®

AuthorHouse™ UK Ltd.
500 Avebury Boulevard
Central Milton Keynes, MK9 2BE
www.authorhouse.co.uk
Phone: 08001974150

First published by AuthorHouse 2/14/2011.

ISBN: 978-1-4567-7427-1 (sc)

To Pauline for the inspiration of ideas and Ellie for inspiring the words.

Chapter 1.

Oh come on , someone is having a laugh at my expense thought Mags when she heard the shout. On your last day as a police officer you are not going to stumble onto a bloody murder just as you are getting ready to say your farewells. No wonder they were so keen on her taking the new recruit for a walk round the patch, and she thought that it was so they could get things ready for the" do" as they called it. Some "do" if she has to be polite and smile at some of that lot. Friends, colleagues and bastards was how she usually regarded them.

Her thoughts were disturbed sharply when the voice of young Sara cut through the clouds in her head. "Sarge", the voice shrieked, " that woman over there has just yelled that there is a body on the floor of the antique shop". The voice faded slightly as the sound of running feet took over. That was the trigger that jolted Sergeant Margaret Woods from her musings about retirement. Don't they teach these youngsters anything these days, why the hell do we have training, her brain screamed at her. Her voice then took over. " Slow it down, stand still, wait!", she shouted in that well practised tone that gave no room for question or challenge. This was the, I am in control and it gets done my way Margaret leaping back into action. " We walk calmly towards the problem young lady, we keep an eye out for any danger and we assess the situation as we move forward", she continued and they walked purposefully forward towards

1

the shop. As they moved closer Mags made sure that Sara understood that rushing in might ruin a crime scene , or worse an intruder could still be there to add to the tally of bodies. No-one knew better than her that killing a police officer can lead to internet fame these days and she wasn't giving anyone a chance to make either of them just another statistic.

" Right", she barked, " talk to the lady who called out and get every detail you can". " Not just name and address, but time, what she saw, the full works, pages of notes if you have to... and don't let any of the public get near" . Mags Woods, for she much preferred that to Margaret, glanced at the scene and took in as much as she could in one swift movement. She could clearly see through the open door that there was the body of a man sprawled in a heap to the side of a display case. There appeared to be some broken glass or something by his head but certainly no sign of anyone else. That needed checking immediately and she prepared to approach the door. Since she had excelled in the unarmed combat course, several years ago, she had always hoped that she could use her skills properly just once, but the chance never came. Well it almost did a couple of years ago at some conference, when the clown who thinks he is the star of CID tried patting her bottom. The look of surprise on his face was a joy to behold as he hit the carpet with a thud and a voice loudly announced that if touched her again he would lose the use of his legs and possibly his manhood at the same time. She had enjoyed that, especially as some men have the charm and charisma of a pig sty after a monsoon , and he was definitely one of that lot. Not that she disliked men, far from it, there had been a few and some of them had style, manners and could actually be trusted. She quite liked men but didn't fancy owning one.

As she called out a warning she carefully entered the shop. All was still except for the increasing beat of her heart, which was drumming away merrily inside her uniform. If this bugger gets up and shouts fooled you then he gets a kicking where he will remember it, wherever he limps she thought. The body was motionless and she reached to seek a pulse. Nothing ,a voice in her head announced and he is quite cold, looks we have a murder on our hands after all. Maybe those silly sods in the station are not roaring with laughter after all this is a live one. Or to be accurate a dead one!

Professionalism took over instantly. " Sara call an ambulance now", she called back through the door," one male about 70 almost certainly dead" . She sensed the excited gasp from outside as she spoke. " What good is an ambulance if he is already dead ?", an enquiring voice replied and so Mags stepped closer and gave her one of the famous Margaret Woods stares. It did not take long to explain that neither of them were qualified to declare death, even if they were certain and the body will be off to the mortuary once the processes got under way. She then began her initial assessment of the scene. Little evidence of break in as the door frame and the lock were intact. The till was firmly shut and there were few visible gaps in the cabinets and glass counter to suggest missing items. Unlikely to be a robbery gone wrong she thought, but now is the time to call it in and hand over to CID. As long as they don't send- he who thinks he is god's gift to women, this should an easy handover she thought. The two of them had history as they say, and on her very last day, there might be some small pleasure in fixing him once and for all, but there was a crime to solve a criminal to find and he couldn't find a parked car even if it was the only one in the car park. This private war began many years ago when they were both on the beat and he had suggested a quick one. She knew instantly he was not talking drinks in the pub at the end of the shift, and besides he always insisted on calling her Margaret, even though he knew full well she hated it. Yes her name was Margaret, but it was only used by her mother, when she had been caught misbehaving, a frequent occurrence, and the sound of" Margaret" brought back too many memories of sins from the past. A few brief words on the radio and the cavalry had been summoned. Let them get on with it was her view, as after the dreaded presentation and speeches she would literally be off the case. Bet not one of them thinks to let her know the final outcome or even think for one second that she might be interested. You never know, perhaps young Sara will be so full of a murder on her first day that she will be unable to resist passing messages on. Must make sure the kid knows how to contact me she thought, that would solve that problem.

With Sara going through her mind, the mother hen sergeant in her kicked in. She stepped into the street to be pleasantly pleased to see all was in good order. The witness was sitting quietly on a little wall a few yards away, crowd control, well, the three or four oddballs just standing and looking, were well back and Sara appeared to be in command of the exterior. "Well done", pronounced Mags, "all under control I see". She ushered Sara a discreet few steps away from prying ears and began to outline her thoughts. Elderly man dead for sure, but how and why, not so sure. Little evidence of robbery unless, when the till is opened, it is empty. She knew little about antiques but a lot of the stuff looked expensive and the odd price tag she had spotted certainly told a story of lots of cash. Some of the stuff in there is priced in thousands she explained so you wouldn't need to take much to be well off if you knew what to take. Mind you that vase thing by his head could have been anything, but heavy it wasn't, so it is unlikely that it was the proverbial blunt instrument. It might squash a fly or a spider , but not much chance of killing a man with it, headache at best she thought. Whilst they exchanged ideas and brought each other up to date a patrol car pulled up and colleagues came to assist. Mags demanded to know who it was on their way from CID and was relieved to hear that her worst fear was not going to be realised. Apparently superstud was heavily involved in some meaningless misdemeanour, which he was blowing out of all proportion as usual. The friends and colleagues part of the friends, colleagues and bastards were keen to assume control to enable their much respected sergeant to get back and prepare for the end of shift festivities. Mags was, however, less than enthusiastic at that prospect and was determined to hang on as long as possible. Serve them right if she did not get back in time but then there were some she did want to say goodbye to properly so it was a no choice job really. "Once CID are here and I can brief them, I will get back, she insisted, " and I will take young Sara with me". " You lot have a good young officer here and if you don't look after her you will have me to answer to cos she has my phone number, so watch your step". No sooner had that been said than the cavalry arrived. Mags was thrilled because as he stepped out of his car she beamed to show her delight. Andy had been on her watch a few years ago, one of the friends, and no-one was more proud than she when he moved over to CID. She refused to call it moving up as that would suggest they were superior and she would never concede there was anything better than being a uniformed officer. They might hang out on the first floor but that was as far up as she would ever agree to. Friends stayed downstairs on the watch, colleagues moved smoothly between both levels and the bastards got to sit in the roof!

Chapter 2.

When the two of them strolled across the rear car park, officers appeared from out of the woodwork to see them. Friends and colleagues alike mingled and chatted and made silly jokes about a murder on the very last shift. Sara shone as if she was the cat that got the cream but Mags was already rehearsing the speech she knew she had no option but to make. The same speech she had rehearsed over several weeks and had spend sleepless nights fine tuning and wondering how far she dare go in one or two comments. The boss, as she called, him loved little anecdotes so some obscure tale from her early days was inevitable and bound to be embarrassing. The Guv, however was another matter. Hopeless speaker and a sense of importance that is all out of proportion and he could say anything but at least everyone will know he is going through the motions and sincerity will be in short supply. If only she could think of a witty, but cutting, remark to make to give all and sundry a chuckle! Two hours to go, a murder to solve and an increasing sense of panic. There was something in the back of her mind about the murder that would not come to the front, something that seemed odd, strange or maybe just out of place. Once forensics and a post mortem are completed all will be clear. At least it will not be her problem someone else can sort it out. No-one wants to have to deal with a major crime on their last day. A killer went into an antique shop, smashed a small pot vase thing over his head, murdered him, took whatever it was he took, and disappeared without any witness. Nice lady who called the police over but she was only passing on her way to the supermarket and frankly did not see a thing. Actually the only thing she did see, other than the body, was two police officers strolling along. Not even CID could pin it on those two, or they had better not suggest it or they will all walk with a permanent limp.

Chapter 3.

Mags sat quietly in her room, her mind was mixing up thoughts of the presentation and the antique shop and very little seemed to make sense or come into any shape or order. Her best uniform was freshly cleaned, her hair carefully brushed, sprayed and ready for the off, and even a little make up was applied, more for comfort than as a statement of anything. Her solitude was interrupted by a knock on the door and she turned to find Sara standing there. " Sorry, but can I have a word before things get under way"?", she enquired. Before Mags could answer Sara started firing on all cylinders. Her big concern was that as the investigation proceeded she would be called upon as the officer first on the scene. A murder on your first day is a massive shock to the system and she was unsure how she would handle it. Her view was that the killer had been disturbed going through the antiques and the shopkeeper got it trying to protect his business.

"Look love", Mags began, " there are a number of possibilities, none of which we have enough information about, but the odds are you are right"

She then went on to offer the possibility that there was little evidence of a robbery because only one item had been taken. After all amongst all that stuff it would be almost impossible to spot one item that was missing, and one or two of those items could have a very big price tag. It seemed to Mags that there was much more to this than met the eye. Assuming only one item was taken then how do you work out what it was and more importantly, why was it taken. Not much chance of digging through a stock list or paperwork to check against what was still there. Some of these dealers are very skilled at not leaving a trail of all their stock. At that thought the lightening of possible realisation hit her. She quickly explained to Sara that perhaps the antique dealer was holding something for someone and when he would not hand it over, because he knew the real value, it all got out of hand. That someone did the deed, took the item and was gone before anyone saw a thing.

" Tell you what young lady", he said, " I bet you that when the dust has settled the killer will be someone the dealer knew".

"Think along those lines and you will have it solved before CID have finished scratching their arses", she laughed, feeling very pleased with her turn of phrase.

" Anyway you sod off, give me a few minutes to get myself ready and keep well away from the wandering hands of that bugger I told you about".

In a few moments the Boss would be along to escort her into the function area, so she took a few slow and purposeful breaths. Feeling calm and a little more relaxed she determined that she would be sweetness and charm itself, accept the jokes and comments with good grace and keep smiling at everyone. Much as she would have loved to have a go at one or two it really wasn't the time or the place and in truth she should have done it ages ago when she was defining friends, colleagues and bastards. Well the bastards anyway.

A few moments later she entered the room with the Boss walking quietly beside her. Comforting that, he had been a good friend for a long time and she respected him, even admired him. Everyone in the room stood and applause filled the air as she was led to a small table at the front. To one side was a row of highly ranked officers and amongst the crowd around her as she walked she noticed a smattering of colleagues from years ago. How nice to think they had dragged themselves out of their retirement leisure to be there to wish her well.

The Boss raised an arm and the room fell silent. The command the man had, she thought, glad he is one of the friends and colleagues. "Friends and colleagues", he said in a deep penetrating voice well known to all of them. " This is a moment when we have come together to wish a much respected colleague, good health and fortune as she embarks upon the journey into retirement". " Mags Woods , and yes I call her Mags because that how she prefers to be addressed, has been an inspiration to many of us". "Everyone in this room knows that she has been a dedicated officer, who would never give up or back down until a problem had been resolved". " Sad in a way that on her very last day she stumbles across a dead body and there is a crime to be solved". "Bet she is already halfway to solving it already so CID had better get a move on, and get it right or she will be back to haunt them!"

Loud and cheery laughter from uniformed ranks was met by only the odd smile. One or two of those odd smiles were also met with dark looks and slight shakes of heads.

"I remember", the Boss continued" many years ago when Mags and I worked closely together".

"Oh God here comes the anecdote, what has he dragged up from the past, but then there was plenty to choose from".

" I recall as if it was yesterday that glorious time when we were called to a disturbance in The Boars Head".

" Drunks everywhere, fists flying and hardly room to raise and arm to protect yourself"

The Boss went on to tell of his and Mags' arrival and how he wondered how he could protect her in the middle of all that mayhem. He need not have worried because Mags stepped into the worst of the fighting and yelled at what appeared to be the two ring leaders. They paused for a moment and stared at the young WPC. She told them in no uncertain terms that if they did not stop at once she would sort them out there and then. They shouldn't have laughed in her face. She calmly picked up a full pint glass and gently poured it over the head of one of them. The other was so busy laughing he did not see her pick up a second pint, and reach for his belt. As she pulled his trousers away from his beer bloated stomach she poured the contents into his trousers. The whole place stood still and frozen. The mayhem was over and everyone knew it. Of course when the tale got round there was an enquiry, but neither of the two men were prepared to make a complaint and insisted on making a formal apology, which effectively meant that was the end of that.

"So, any of you who have really upset dear Mags over the years, I strongly recommend that you be sure only to drink shorts or you may be dripping from your turn ups for the rest of the evening", he said with some relish.

"So, my dear friend and colleague Mags, this is the moment when you take your final bow". "Our service will be the lesser for your departure but a chance to take it easy, prune roses and attack retail therapy with enthusiasm, is rightly earned". "If by any chance you have solved the antiques job by the morning do please give one of my team a call, they might need all the help they can get". " Don't expect the credit for it but with a bit of luck you might get thanked"

"Before the formal presentation I have one little task to perform and I know how much you will appreciate it". " I have here an envelope for you, just a little token from me personally". All those years ago when you stopped seeing that nice young doctor from the hospital you told me you had a career in front of you and sex was not on the agenda, so I present to you a packet of condoms so you can make up for lost time safely".

The whole room burst into a riot of laughter, the loudest roars coming from Mags herself. She could not resist reaching forward and kissing him on the cheek, and was met by a face that lit up at her touch.

" Sorry old friend but you will have to join the queue if you think that you will be first in line when I give them a test run!".

Friends dabbed their eyes as tears of laughter welled , shoulders pumped up and down like pistons and they were the lead in a spontaneous burst of applause. Colleagues grinned, chuckled and smirked at each other, she never let them down with the quick remark. The bastards stood in stunned silence, with looks that said- inappropriate-but forced smiles to show that they were not completely out of touch or lacking in humour.

As the Guv moved to the centre front the room fell silent. "Margaret Woods has been a fine officer, a loyal colleague and a good example to us all", he intoned.

A voice in Mags' head softly muttered. " Damn him he knows Margaret is never used, did it on purpose, thinks it makes him look all formal and important, my day not his, remember calm and keep smiling" A forced smile passed across her face but those who knew her well could see the traces of tension hidden there.

The Guv went on and on about nothing in particular, most of it being about his team, his career and his, this that and the other. He just had to mention that he was the officer in charge of the disciplinary hearing over the beer down the trousers incident. Oh how deadly serious it all was, risk to a blossoming career, such sadness at one lapse that ruin future promotion. How delighted he was when so unexpectedly the two drunks concerned demanded to withdraw any complaints and even turned up to present personal letters of apology to the officer. Unheard of but so very welcome.

" Insincere bastard", the brain quietly muttered .

As the Guv droned on and on, the boss whispered in Mags's ear. He had sought out the two of them, explained a few home truths and set up the withdrawl and the formal apology. They had been told if the matter went ahead it would be the personal mission of the whole station to make their lives absolute hell. Pass wind in a public place and you will find yourself arrested for something they were told. They were cornered and quickly did as they were told knowing the consequences were too much to consider.

The private whisperings came to an abrupt halt when at long last the moment of presentation was reached. A formal hand over of several gifts, a handshake and it was all over, much to the relief of the whole room who were wilting by this time and besides the bar was being opened. Thank God he didn't try and kiss me thought Mags, I might have bitten off his ear!

Speech! Speech! Echoed around the room andMags knew that here was the moment she was dreading most. Still, big smile deep breath and keep it short and polite, just as rehearsed.

"Thank you all for being here to wish me well as I move quietly off towards the sunset", began Mags." To see so many faces from the past touches me greatly, and of course current colleagues are here in abundance". So glad to see that you can still laugh at my jokes even if they are slightly, well you know what I mean". " References to my little altercation in the Boars Head, all those years ago brought back so many memories". " If any of you had heard what they actually said to me, then you would have understood why I reacted so swiftly and I admit unprofessionally". " None of that of course would have come out if the internal enquiry had gone ahead, sorry sir, but a quick sweep under the carpet, suspend and show how clean we are was order of the day". "Nowadays it would have been trial by media which in some ways is probably worse".

"Now is the time for me take a rest, enjoy the garden that has been crying out for attention for a very long time and maybe get a dog and do a little walking". "When thinking about what I might say to you I was determined to keep it brief but to at least share with you all a few thoughts". "Bear in mind, all of you, that the youngsters joining the force today are the future of the service". "Look after them and treat them as you would your own family". "I went walkabout with a young lady today and she will surprise you all I am sure". "Give her a chance and she will sort out the death at the antique shop, she is almost all the way there now". "CID listen to her, she has a wise head on her shoulders, don't use your usual trick of thinking that you alone solve major crimes". "As for the upper echelons of the force, well I said brevity was the order of the day, so support your staff fully for without them you would have nothing to manage, organise or respond to your latest brainwaves". "I have had a wonderful career amongst real friends and colleagues and I thank you for all of it". "Finally when I get to the bottom of today's events, and I actually thought it was you lot having a laugh at my expense, I will quietly let you know, but be warned the credit and information will go where it will be best deserved". "Thank you for being here, goodnight and yes I would love a drink at the bar!"

The room erupted in a crescendo of shouts and applause, leaving Mags standing with a slightly bemused expression on her face.

Chapter 4

He sat alone in his chair with just his thoughts for company. Grief is a dark place, a veritable goulash of emotion that sweeps in like a sea mist, till the damp fingers of reality wrap themselves around the mind and squeeze relentlessly. He had loved her with every ounce of his being, but the fates had decreed that she should go. Whilst she was in hospital care there was always hope, even though that was a very slender thread upon which to hold on to a future. She had always said she wished to go first as she could not see how she would cope without him, and she regarded him as a survivor, someone who could rebuild a life. She lived to make him happy, and he her, but she had made sure he understood that she expected him to hopefully find a new life, one of happiness and joy such as they had shared. No comfort, however, when sitting in a chair and feeling the waves of sadness, loneliness and simple misery pour over him. He sat and reflected on their life together, trying in his mind to reassure himself that he had done all that he could, that he, as promised all those years ago, had provided, protected and defended her, to the death if necessary.

Duncan met his beloved Helen as children at school. They were the best of friends and he was happy to bring some laughter and some purpose into her rather sad childhood existence. The boys at school did not make remarks or call out to Helen, as they did to the other girls because the older Duncan was in the background and he would have stepped in fast. If you asked him why he was protective of this little girl he would shrug his shoulders and tell them he wasn't sure but he felt protective and that is what she got. As the years progressed they became ever closer, with the young Helen, by the time she was only thirteen, confiding in him, sharing her deepest thoughts and illustrating unhappy times in her short life. This may well have been a trigger that opened up their future together, even if they did not realise it. They would meet up in the park or on the promenade and sit and simply share each thought and experience. Duncan explained how he had fought to overcome the trauma and disadvantage of being confined in a hospital bed from the age of five until he was almost ten. She loved the way he would dismiss sympathetic comments with a smile and a quick joke. " Unfortunately I can't blame it on the war" he said," my own fault really, too young to understand what danger was". She admired the way that he had a clear view of what he wanted in life and an even clearer view of how it could be achieved. " That's what comes from being in a ward with all the old men, because I was not allowed to move about or be active". He had few friends as so many of the others found him far too serious and not inclined to join in lively youthful antics. Indeed he disapproved openly, which did not make him particularly popular, although one or two loyal friends tried their best to involve him in their lives.

Helen would sit and chatter away, feeling safe and relaxed, as she talked about her life. Her alcoholic father was a massive problem, always rows and trouble at home. He would roll in from the local pub, fall in a heap on the settee and snore loudly for the rest of the evening. She did not want to bring friends to her home and let them see that. Neither parent ever asked about school, did not attend parent evenings to check on progress and she was well used to signing her reports on their behalf and handing the slip back in a school the next morning. The school would never have known because she wrote her own absence notes as and when they were needed. Duncan winced in horror when he was told that at the time she had her first show in puberty her mothers' response was to complain about the expense and proceeded to make towels out of old material and cotton wool then gave her safety pins to attach to her underwear. His brain raced around as to how he could buy what she needed so that she would have some dignity, but found that he could not find the words to make such an offer. He understood the mechanics but struggled with the emotions. One evening as they sat and chatted away Helen broke into the conversation with a startling revelation. Duncan was so taken aback, feeling completely out of his depth that he instinctively put a protective arm around her shoulder. She nestled closer and they sat in reflective silence. After a few minutes Duncan removed his arm and found himself apologising for manhandling her as he put it. Her response was to take the arm and place it carefully back to where it had been. That evening as he walked her home she took his hand and squeezed it gently. At the end of the road by her house she moved close and gave him a gentle kiss on the cheek. He smiled, she grinned and the mutually dependent friendship had begun the path to love and romance. From that day they shared every thought, every plan and a future together started to be slowly mapped out.

Now all alone Duncan reached deep into his mind, seeking comfort, for surely he had given all that he could, all that they had planned, all that they had seen as their dearest wish. A home, a comfortable life, a family, but above all a devotion that lasted all her life. Her faithful companion, steadfast by her side, she steering gently as only she knew how, was now alone. The family had been a tower of strength as he fought to face the world again and he had a determination to ensure that the grand plan, put in place all of fifty years ago by two children, came to fruition. The children were settled, she was thrilled at that, and now the grandchildren were the centre focus as she had always intended. Grandmothers did not come more proud than Helen.

Duncan had one deep regret and still he battled with it even now. In all those years together they shared everything, held no secrets and were as one as it is possible to be. However, and there is always an however, there was one detail that Duncan had never told his beloved Helen. He could never find the words to tell her, nor find the courage to share anything about one event in their lives together. He wasn't ashamed, no he actually felt pride, but he just could not bring himself to tell her. The risk of her being hurt was just too great. He had summoned up the courage to tell her as she lay in the hospital and had planned how he would do it. It was too late; for that was the day that the alarms rang out, medics rushed around and he heard the words he dreaded hearing.

" We tried everything we could but I am sorry we could not save her"

Chapter 5.

When the phone rang Mags was just finishing the washing up. After a busy career she now found that the basic household tasks cluttered up her life. When she was working, the washing, the ironing, dusting and tidying somehow magically were done as and when she had a few moments. Now it seemed as if they were carefully planned and fitted a schedule. Strange that she thought, anyone would think that in retirement you did as you pleased. Well it just wasn't true, each task needed its time in the day and this robotic routine annoyed her. She really wasn't like that! The phone jolted her out of her thoughts and she reached out to answer.

" Its' me, Sara, I've got some news and it makes the mystery even stranger," the voice said.

"Slow down, slow down, give me a second, now what are you going on about?"

Sara went on to explain that new information now made the death at the antique shop a bit of a puzzle. There was lots to tell and it would take too long on the phone so she suggested that they might meet for a coffee and then she could bring Mags up to date .

This news was just what Mags needed to brighten up her day and they very quickly made arrangements. Fortunately Sara was on an early shift so she would be free in the early afternoon. With news of developments on offer Mags was free anytime. The little coffee shop at the end of the precinct was an ideal meeting place because it had several alcoves and tables where you could have a bit of privacy. The perfect place to spill the beans and tell all.

After she had put the phone down Mags muttered one of her favourite oaths and scratched her head. Something has happened, there is some news, and not one of them bothered to let her know. Well not exactly not one of them because Sara was ready willing and able to do just that. Mags knew she was not wrong when she put her faith in Sara and passing on her phone number had been a good move. At long last some progress and another crime solved, unless the news is that some clown has made a mess of it and it is all back to square one. She quickly organised herself and was soon ready to head into the town to meet Sara. She wanted to get there early as she could take the opportunity to pick up a few things in the shops on the way.

With the car safely parked in the car park Mags made her way out to street level. A few shoppers were wandering around, a couple were arguing outside one of the stores but not a lot was happening. She then realised that old habits die hard and what she was actually doing was assessing the scene and committing it to memory. She smiled to herself at that. Whatever she might have believed she had seen there were things that somehow had locked themselves into her mind. Now locked away for future use, or not as the case might be, was the lady with the guide dog puppy on its training walk; the youth with the baseball cap, turned backwards of course, huddled in the corner by the cash machine; the couple with enough holiday brochures to sink the cruise ship rather than travel on it; the elderly man sitting alone by the litter bin just staring into space; the young mother with the pushchair who didn't look old enough to be a parent. The list just went on and on.

As she approached the coffee shop she could see Sara waiting there and thought how good she looked out of uniform. Casual clothes suited her and she had the figure to show off the latest fashion and style. They greet rather formally and hurried inside, with Sara moving quickly to a convenient table out of the way and Mags heading to the counter to get the drinks. A few moments later a tray of steaming coffee was placed on the table and they sat down both eager to share and hear the latest news. A quick glance told them that the coffee shop was almost empty and so there was little chance that they would be overheard.

"Right, what's going on?, asked Mags in an urgent voice. There was an excitement in her tone as she urged Sara to begin. " Don't keep me waiting, I am dying to know how right I was"

" Well," said Sara, trying to keep her own voice calm and matter of fact. "It's like this you see", and off she went on a long explanation of the news she had gathered.

" The old boy died of a heart attack, but he had a bruise on the side of his head and another just under his arm"

"The suggestion is that he must have fallen or was pushed so that he caught his head and side on the counter"

"No traces of the broken vase in the wound so it must have been knocked as he fell"

"The mob upstairs think whatever happened scared him so much he had a heart attack and keeled over" .

"No news about anything missing, but it could be just one item like you said because when they examined the books and his records there were all sorts of things that did not add up".

" A couple of items in the shop were on a list of stuff stolen years ago so it is almost certain he was on the fiddle and up to something".

"The clever lot are looking into his affairs cos so much seems to be unrecorded"

"They reckon the tax man will want to look into him very closely, he certainly wasn't the nice little old antiques chap everyone thought he was"

Sara went on to explain that the general thoughts were that he had been scared into a heart attack. A robbery was a possibility, but less likely than a disagreement over one item in the shop. As the old man obviously traded around the edges of the law he could easily be involved in something illegal. One suggestion being followed is along the lines of something pretty valuable had been left in the shop as a storage facility, until things had quietened down, and the old fool has sold it on. One of the team is digging into records to check on high value goods that have never been traced. The inspector liked this idea, even though it may well mean manslaughter rather than murder.

" He bloody would", interrupted Mags, " anything that gets him all the publicity. " You see even if it is only manslaughter it will probably lead to the solving of a major theft or fraud and we all know who will be giving all the TV interviews". " You might think that murder is a high profile job, but there is just as much promotional mileage in the clearing up of a crime involving vast sums of money". " The media love those

, lots of spins offs and other avenues that can be dragged in to make a good story".

The two of them sat, sipping coffee, trawling through possibilities and playing the guesswork game for all they were worth. The conversation paused when Mags suddenly asked if Sara had spotted the scruffy youth by the cash point in the precinct, puffing away on a cigarette. Sara did not have a clue what she was talking about. Mags went on to explain that she noticed him as she made her way to the coffee shop from the car park. It had aroused her interest because there was something odd about him. She had suddenly asked the question because she saw him moving away from his corner looking around as he went.

The youth was not sufficiently interesting to occupy them for more than a few seconds, there were more important things to talk about. Now that Sara had passed on all she could about events since the retirement, all she could focus upon was hopefully words of wisdom that she felt sure would gently fall upon her like a summer shower. Mags did not disappoint.

" Well, well, well" ,she began. " Not a lot changes does it?" " They could well be on the right track but I still have a funny feeling that they are charging off in a direction that will lead them nowhere". " The idea of a Mr.Big hiding stuff down here for a few years till the heat is off sounds as if it comes straight from the pages of a cheap novel or some afternoon television drama". Possible, you can't discount it, but you know I think they should be thinking differently instead of the usual straight lines". " I am not able to explain it, but, I just feel that the dodgy dealing is only part of the story". "A close look into the man's life might be more rewarding, because there is something there that could have scared him to death". " Could be crossing a criminal mastermind, but what if it is something else entirely?

Sara listened intently nodding her head. That idea had not even occurred to her, but yes it was possible. It could be easier to find something in his life that could cause a heart attack rather than hunt for an antique that may or may not exist, may or may not be incredibly valuable and no one knows if it was stolen in the first place. The big, "but", to all that was that he appears to have been a very ordinary man, nothing particularly special about him, well liked, popular except for some dubious stock in his shop. Give him the benefit of the doubt that he did not know and he becomes, well, of no interest really.

The meeting had to come to an end as the staff in the coffee shop began wiping the tables and made a point of swinging the closed sign on the door. The final hint was one of them putting on her coat and announcing that she would see everyone in the morning. Mags and Sara agreed to meet up again at a later date, yet to be settled, and they made their ways outside. A few brief words and they went their separate ways.

Chapter 6

Out in the cool air Mags looked around, as she always did. The youth had gone, the last few shoppers were heading home and a small queue formed by the car park machine waiting to pay. Another young mum hurried by and Mags began to feel old, these Mums are so young she thought, heavens they start early these days. As she reached the end of the little queue she reached for her purse and took out the coins that she would need. As she did so she spotted out of the corner of her eye the elderly man still sitting by the litter bin. Poor old soul she thought, he is in no hurry to go home and must be stiff if he has been sitting there all this time. She made a mental note that it was all very well going on about young mums and pushchairs and stuff, but someone ought to spare a thought for the elderly who for whatever reason just sit out and the world revolves around them. The thought, that she was at least not one of them, yet, was accompanied by a deep sigh.

Car park fee paid, exit ticket stamped and she was all ready to go. She made her way to the car and got in. Against the far wall of the leant the youth from the cash machine. She looked at him for a few moments and decided that she had better let her former friends know about him, because if they did not know of him, they certainly will, for he was a crime statistic waiting to happen. Handbag snatches, that sort of thing, yes he is bound to be someones' wanted list and a whole bundle of paperwork can be tied up with a nice ribbon. One up for uniform if she is right, and if she was wrong, well she didn't like the look of him anyway!

The car moved steadily into the stream of traffic and Mags was soon on her way home. It seemed like a brilliant idea to look into the antique dealers life but now it seems as if that is a blind alley. He might have been a bit naughty, knowingly or otherwise, but ordinary does not mix comfortably with where her imaginings were taking her. A need to return to the drawing board, perhaps, but her first instincts had always stood her in good stead in the past. Must be a sign of ageing that instincts leave you when you least expect it. Damn, damn, she wondered to herself, this whole business keeps bugging me. For some unknown reason it keeps getting into my head and the bloody thoughts won't go away. She knew it was her last day, she initially thought it was a big joke, but now it was becoming a matter that got in the way of living. She just knew that there was a clue there somewhere but her brain would just not give it up.

Chapter 7.

Days and even weeks were a bit of a blur to Duncan as each one was much the same. He had tried to establish a routine to maintain some kind of structure in life but that proved little consolation. Yes, Mondays were for cleaning and vacuuming upstairs, Tuesdays the down stairs rooms were attacked and Wednesdays were for the kitchen. Thursdays it was the turn of the bathroom and a Friday treat was the washing and the ironing. Wow ,what an exciting life I lead, was his approach, which just about saw him through the dullness of his existence, or survival as he preferred to regard it. Being locked into the routine still left him time for other things but finding other things was another matter. A little shopping for essentials filled the odd hour and he found himself sitting in a good vantage point, or camping out as he called it, and simply watching the world go by. Sometimes he would spot something that would amuse him, but far too many times he saw things that would make him feel old and very grumpy. The newspapers did little to help as he began to feel that he was getting out of touch with the world around him.

He watched very young Mums with their babies, the very same ones that Mags had observed, but they did not make him smile. The papers would have stories of youngsters some under sixteen, who were out at the clubs and parties and falling over in the street, awash with alcohol, and that puzzled him. Who the bloody hell was at home looking after the children!

Still the bench in the shopping mall was slightly out of any breeze and draught so it was not too bad a place to kill and hour or so. There was even the opportunity to pop into one of the coffee bars for a warm drink if needed, but they were rather noisy places with people gossiping away unaware that anyone else was simply seeking a little peace and quiet. From time to time he might spot someone in an outfit that did nothing to flatter their shape, which would cause him to quietly grin to himself but by far the best were the children. A young mother with a demanding child were the perfect example of the destruction of the English language and meaningless statements.

" If you don't shut up you is getting nothing"

"When I tell your dad he will kill you"

"Straight to bed when you get home and then you will be quiet and I won't have to put up with all your moaning, I got a life you know"

As these gems of wisdom swept over the child, another biscuit or piece of cake would be crammed into its mouth. Well a sweet gag is one way of getting silence!

Chapter 8

Mags too had developed a routine, all that training must have paid off, but she also found that being less active and less involved almost painful. She longed to get news from the friends and at least they were quite good at keeping in touch. Young Sara was especially good at that, even if there was never any news of progress on her case. The whole thing is going to end up in a file at the bottom of a filing system gathering dust, because in truth they haven't a clue. Actually that was very accurate, they hadn't, and any initial impetus was fading fast. Death was natural causes, slightly odd circumstances, a few unanswered questions but what the hell, tie a ribbon round it, file it and move on to something else! If you don't make a fuss then there is no case to investigate.

Mags knew full well that detective work had an interesting similarity to sex. There is a lot of painstaking preparation and anticipation; an even greater amount of effort; masses of leg work; and it in some cases goes on and on, seemingly forever! Then when you think that it is all going so wonderfully well , it can fizzle out and leave you feeling deflated.

Heaven's I am becoming a cynical old devil, thought Mags, but then she remembered that in actual fact she always had been. If truth be told she was famous for her cynicism, especially if it involved the bastards in the attic. When she told Sara what she had been thinking, the young officer blushed slightly and began to wonder if she too might slowly find herself wandering down that path. Sara giggled nervously and said," I am dating that young CID officer you spoke so highly of, and yes preparation comes into it, leg work too, but fizzling out...no chance..well not yet anyway"

Mags roared with laughter, it was a tonic talking with Sara, even if there was never any news of progress in the case. Well there was news, and not surprisingly it was simply that it was easier to call it a non-case and put it to bed. Mags had to agree with them, there was little choice, but still way back in the remotest recesses of her mind there was something. That damn something kept hiding there and would not come out to play. One little detail, one tiny item of information, is all that needs to come to the front of the mind and the clouds will lift and hey presto all will be revealed. Fat chance of that when whatever it is stubbornly refuses to budge from its hiding place.

Sara had provided the background that Mags wanted but it did not appear to make much sense. Reginald Morris, was nothing more than a fairly successful antique dealer, who ran an perfectly ordinary shop. Mind you he did give himself a few airs and graces so he probably referred to it as an emporium. He was vice chairman of the local Chamber of Commerce, due almost certainly to be Chairman in a year or so. He was going to stand for the council but somehow he never actually presented the nomination papers, much to the surprise of his circle of friends. A bit odd that, but it can't be all that significant as everyone is entitled to change their mind at the last minute. That is not an offence, well not yet anyway. A few questionable items in the shop is a possible line of enquiry, but the "brains department" have let that go cold, so that is another blind alley. He was married, a daughter with children, but being a grandparent is ordinary not criminal. Sod it, thought Mags it really is just a simple death by natural causes, but why on earth do I keep thinking that there is something that has not been spotted, the key that unlocks what it is all about. She knew deep down that her instincts rarely let her down, and she was not one to fret and worry about things. Fretting and worrying was exactly what she was doing, there was something, she knew it, but it was hiding and refused to let her get her teeth into it. A trip to the shops was the answer, something to take her mind off the whole affair. Retail therapy can be the antidote to all sorts of ills and this wasn't just an ill it was a full blown sickness.

Once in the town Mags, picked up a few items from the shops and decided to have a cup of coffee before heading for home again. At least there was no sign of the youth, they had obviously sorted him out. People passed by the window of the coffee bar, mothers with pushchairs, and elderly ladies struggling with carrier bags. They ought to give a bag on wheels to all pensioners as they retire she thought. What a great idea, until she remembered that if that was the case then she would have one beside her at the table. Stupid things, you won't catch me wheeling one of those about, getting in the way and leaving a purse vulnerable to any sneaky bugger who happens to be on the look- out. Done a few of them in my time, she thought, but they never get the sentence I would have imposed. If I had become a magistrate they would have sacked me for dishing out sentences that were too severe.

As random thoughts flitted across her conscious mind her eyes were drawn to the bench seat tucked in the corner. That poor old chap was sitting there once again, what a life with nothing to do but just sit. Her caring instincts went into overdrive and before she realised it she had finished her coffee, and was boldly marching towards the figure on the bench. As she approached she began to wonder what she was going to actually do. You can't just march up to someone and ask them what they are doing sitting on a seat, not being a nuisance or anything like that. Somehow that did not stop her as her feet kept up the momentum and she found herself looking at him.

He was quite smartly dressed, casual but neat and tidy, but it was the sad and vacant look in his eyes that drew upon all her concern. She glanced at his shoes, you can tell a lot about people from their shoes, perfectly smart, clean and unremarkable. Striking up a conversation with a complete stranger is not easy, especially when all the body language is shouting leave me alone.

" Not so cold today is it?", she found herself saying. Her brain was screaming that the weather is a sorry old conversation starter but it was too late it had been said.

"Not too bad" came the reply, which at least gave a chance for something that might pass as a conversation.

" I've just had a coffee over there and couldn't help noticing that you have been sitting here for ages, is everything alright?"

" Thanks for asking but I am fine, just killing a bit of time before I make my way home"

" Funny that I only came down here for a few bits and pieces to break up the day a bit, on my own you see and sometimes it is nice to be amongst people even, if they are crowds just rushing around"

Mags found herself moving to sit beside this stranger, something was telling her that it was something she should do. He did not react, so she chirpily carried on with the conversation, even though the few words exchanged hardly merited the description of conversation.

" I believe I have seen you on this seat a few times in the past so I assume you come here often"

" Oh god did I really say that, sorry that sounds awful"

"Can't help it you see, I was a police officer until a while ago when I retired, and I spend most of my working life being observant, watching people and trying to be a help"

" That's ok", Duncan replied in a soft and quite cultured voice. " I'm doing nothing really just wasting time and trying to keep out of everyone's way"

" Yes I do a lot of nothing, sometimes I wonder if I do anything else, but I find it tiring".

" Well ,yes you would, because doing nothing is bloody hard work, because you have no way of knowing when you have finished!"

Mags laughed out loud at this remark and out of the corner of her eye she noticed that he too had a gentle grin playing around his mouth. Ice had been broken, she felt a slight buzz, this could be a really nice chap but caution and slowly must be the order of the day. She quickly jumped to her feet and with a brief explanation of the need to get home she began to take her leave.

" I won't intrude any more, nice to have met you, who knows we might meet again on our trips to the town centre"

" Well I am often here on my seat, and who knows if you promise not to go on about police matters I might just offer to take you over there for a coffee"

Chapter 9

Sara James was a good young officer, thoughtful, quick witted and with an eye for detail. Even though she had only worked with Mags Woods for a few hours, some things just seem to rub off. Some things never seem to change either and she had soon found that she had to fend off other officers, especially those upstairs. She had friends and a selection of colleagues, but rarely came across the bastards. After she had accepted a drink after shift offer from Andy in CID, her world began on a track that she had not anticipated. She had known instantly that Mags strongly approved of Andy, she even said so, and so she felt sure that accepting the invite would be at least safe. How right she was. Andy may have been a tall and powerful, rugby mad, man but he also had an aura of kindness and consideration surrounding him. He opened doors for ladies, he ensured that they were properly looked after and did not even push his luck when it came to saying goodnight. Strangely as their friendship developed, looks, comments and remarks, within the station, went from a trickle to a complete stop. When she had told Mags of this closeness, the smile on her face beamed approval. Now she had even bigger news to pass on as she had agreed to move in with Andy. Well, why not, she rarely went to her own flat after an evening out and there were more of her clothes at his place than there were at her own.

Cuddled up with Andy she felt as if there was nothing in the world that would dare harm her. From time to time shift patterns meant that they only met up in the same place for fleeting minutes, but the times when they had a day or a night together they knew how to make up for lost time. Andy had joked that when Mags knew she would be sending round her packet of condoms just in case. Sara laughed at this and vowed to make sure that Mags was told what had been said. Andy pretended horror at the prospect , but was more than confident that Mags would be delighted for both of them, even if she was likely to go on and on about children getting in the way of a career, with plenty of time for all that later.

"Tell you what love", Andy suddenly announced," on our next day off together lets go over to Mags and tell her our plans". " It will be smashing to see her again and we can make a day of it and take her out for a spot of lunch or something"

Sara thought for a few moments, she sensed a Mags lecture on the horizon. A lecture from Mags was always something to look forward to as you never knew what she was likely to say. If Mags decided to shock, just for devilment, then it was as if you had been connected to a power socket.

"Great idea, let's do that as soon as we can, but be warned she will want to question you about the antique shop, like a dog with a bone as far as that is concerned". " Even though all the evidence points in the opposite direction she keeps niggling away at it as if her life depended on it." " I thought at one time she was going to invent a murderer, get him arrested and sort out the details later". " No, it will be nice to see her again, not really the old dragon people thought, but bloody tenacious she definitely is!"

Chapter 10

When Mags got the call from Sara, a great smile enveloped her face. Of course she was not busy; of course she would love to see them; of course she would love to hear some exciting news. She knew instantly that this was personal news and nothing to do with her retirement day. He mind raced around guessing wildly as to the news she was about to be given. Pregnant, no chance, Sara is much too smart for that and Andy is far too caring and supportive to allow that to happen. A wedding, well that is possible, but Mags felt she might just be a little too long in the tooth to be a bridesmaid, matron of honour might be ok, but the word honour worried her because you can never be sure what that might involve. Well something is happening and its personal, and it sounds as if everyone is excited. The thought of a promotion and a move flicked into her mind, but she dismissed that quickly because surely someone would have let her know that such a thing was in the pipeline.

No, she decided, she would just have to be patient and wait till they arrived. Mags quickly changed into an outfit suitable for going out for a meal, even if it was almost certainly going to be in the pub. She waved a brush at her hair, patted it down and pronounced to the mirror that she would do. As she looked around her home she felt a surge of domesticity. A quick tidy would not go amiss. Picking up discarded newspapers, straightening a few cushions and a mad rush at the bathroom followed in quick succession.

A further glance and the vacuum cleaner was out from the cupboard under the stairs. Boldly marching up and down, the whirring machine leading the way, the carpets soon gave up the odd items discarded and looked fresh and inviting. Next for the treatment was the kitchen, a rapid wipe of surfaces, a rinse of the sink and draining board and all was close to ready. She gathered the better mugs from the cupboard, the ones on the stand were a bit past their best, and laid them out for a coffee upon arrival. Once the kettle was filled and ready to go, she breathed a heavy sigh of relief that all was well and presentable. Mags, the career girl was turning into a fussy domestic soul, who even spent time putting cushions in exactly the right place, whereas usually they were thrown , at least they did in the world of Margaret Woods. As she bent her knees slightly to park herself in her chair the door bell rang signalling the arrival of Sara and Andy. Mags had promised herself she would be very matter of fact, smile broadly and wait patiently to hear the news whatever it was. With that in mind she straightened up and walked purposefully to the door.

Chapter 11

"If you've got her pregnant, I will rip your bits off with my bare hands!", she shouted as she flung open the door.

The postman looked rather taken aback at this but determinedly pushed forward a large brown envelope and requested a signature.

" Sorry, oh, er, sorry, thought you were someone else" spluttered Mags trying desperately not to blush.

"Well whoever he is ,it sounds as if he is going to get more than a signature!". "God help him when he gets here"

" Actually he is walking up behind you", Mags said trying to sound calm and matter of fact.

" Well I am off before the blood gets spilled".

Andy was puzzled as he approached the door and the words of the postman were spinning round in his head.

" You dirty sod, I'd run for it whilst you've got the chance if I were you mate!"

Hugs and greetings and the two were ushered in to the safety of the hallway and the door was firmly shut behind them.

" Got a problem with the postman?", enquired Andy as he lowered himself into an armchair.

" No not really, a simple case of mistaken identity" laughed Mags as she scurried into the kitchen to make coffee. At least in there he would not be asking more questions and she had a respite to gather her thoughts and her composure. If you are going to put your foot in it, then jump right in!

With the best mugs brimming with coffee and everyone seated Mags could contain herself no longer. All her good intentions of being patient went flying away.

" Right you two, what is the exciting news?".

" Well", Andy began, "before you ask Sara is not pregnant".

"I'll kill that bloody postman"

"What has the postman got to do with anything? " Sara quietly asked.

Andy wasn't a detective for nothing and was beginning to add up in his head as fast as he could. Within a split second he had worked out that Mags had greeted the poor chap thinking it was them. What a golden opportunity to rag her without mercy, a chance in a life time to get one over on the much loved Mags. He did not waste a precious second and accused her of assuming a pregnancy and chasing after ideas with no facts to go on. Mags took it on the chin as she knew she would have to, and Andy was a dear friend so if anyone is allowed to get away with it he was. Well he was allowed the liberty till he made a fatal mistake. When you overplay your hand it can come back to bite you. When he raised the matter of the antique shop and assumptions with no facts to go on red rags and bulls flew into the equation. The second he said it he knew the thin ice was cracking and he blurted an apology as swiftly as he could get his tongue round the words. Mags was a loyal friend and accepted willingly, but insisted that they return to the subject after she had received the major news.

Sara relayed the news that she and Andy were now properly a couple and had decided to move in together. They had talked it through and it made a lot of sense. Their friendship had moved from simply that to a closeness that was now love. They wanted Mags to be the first to know and Mags was flattered that they thought of her as important in their lives. Sara also, as she told Andy she would, mentioned the remark about the condoms and Mags rocked with laughter.

" Well you can whistle for those", she chuckled," I have some news for you and I might just need them myself!"

Andy looked at Sara and she responded with a gaping mouth and a sharp intake of breath. For a moment or two they just looked at each other in stunned silence. Mags just had to be joking and pulling their legs; Mags had news and clearly this was a man in life, a wild passion that had been a very carefully kept secret.

"Tell all" a breathless Sara demanded," what is his name, who is he ,what does he do, how did you meet, come on come on tell!"

Mags took a deep breath.

"Now I don't want you to get all silly and that", began Mags ", there isn't much to tell"

"I met this man near the coffee bar when out shopping. " He is elderly but there is something about him that drew me to him even though I don't know his name or anything much about him"

" Bloody hell you need the condoms for a chap you picked up in the street, we arrest women for soliciting you know", Andy couldn't resist saying.

" Yes, yes, very funny but you have got it all wrong".

" I saw him sitting all alone and just felt the need to see if all was well".

"We talked for a few moments and I felt that I needed to get to know him better, not sex, not all that stuff, just an unexplained feeling that drew me to him"

"Although he was surrounded by sadness there was a little spark of a smile in his eyes and I just wanted to know more"

" You might be too young, but I can tell you at my age there can be a moment, one you can't even explain to yourself, when something just feels right and worthwhile." "That is when you find yourself realising how remote from the world you have allowed yourself to become, and that there are things out there to be seized and enjoyed, like friendship, companionship and who knows maybe love"

The rarely swearing Sara just looked open eyed and muttered , "bloody hell!"

Mags went on to explain that they had only met once, did not even know each other's names or for that anything about each other, but there was something, just something that was calling on her to follow wherever it might lead her. The two youngsters sat in amazement as Mags informed them that there was every chance that when she and this stranger met next time they might go for a coffee and simply chat.

" Well" said Andy, " I thought we had exciting news, but you have topped that Mags"

" The Boss was only saying the other day that you could surprise us all even yet and you certainly have done that"

" If you mention a word of this to anyone you will get a surprise visit in hospital from my postman, and you can work out that one for yourself"

Andy knew what she was saying and swore an oath of silence and total discretion.

The meal in the pub was a riot of laughter as the conversation swung from behaving like rabbits, to tall dark strangers, back to condoms and dates over coffee. Other customers enjoying a quiet drink or a bite to eat must have been greatly amused to see the three of them grinning, laughing and waving arms about like a group of teenagers escaped from school.

The light hearted mood only took on a serious tone when Andy took the courage to mention the death at the antique shop. He knew he would have to and the sooner any awkwardness was out of the way the better. Gently he explained that every avenue they had explored came to a dead end, no facts to do much about and really that was the end of the matter officially. Sometimes a case goes like that, Mags knew that full well, and now there were more urgent matters demanding attention. Unless something staggering comes to light then the matter is simply done and dusted. The family are satisfied, the legal brains are satisfied and the top floor are glad to chalk up another tidy statistic and move on. He felt pleased with his little speech as Mags had listened carefully and thoughtfully.

" You are right Andy, I have other things to occupy my mind now, my mystery lover so to speak, but all I would say is that we all missed something, but if everyone is happy ,what the hell".

Chapter 12

The week went slowly by and Mags had busied herself in the house. There are always little jobs to be done and yet when she was working full time they rarely showed themselves. Little flickers of guilt dodged around in her thoughts as she pottered about. All these little routine things must have been there all the time, but were simply ignored, but now they stood up and demanded her attention. She consoled herself with the thought that every now and again she had had a tidy and cleaning day and that must have kept everything in check. Now with plenty of time to do chores they just presented themselves by standing to attention. None of this prevented her from letting her imagination have a free reign, and she needed little excuse to organise herself to take a trip to the town. Of course there were a few odds and ends that would come in handy, but there was just the remote possibility that the gentleman might be sitting in his usual place. An opportunity to remind him of the coffee offer and to find out a little more about him.

As she came from the car park she looked across to the seat. It was empty, no sign, and a feeling of almost disappointment swept over her. She could not explain to herself why she should feel this way but there was no escaping from the fact that is exactly how she felt. There were odds and ends to be got so she began to drift in and out of a variety of shops, collecting a few pieces as she went. The jolt she felt as she emerged from the chemists was something she could not remember feeling ever before. There on the seat was the figure of her mystery man! Sure enough he was in his usual place, her little plan was coming together.Excitedly, rather like a schoolgirl on her first date, she skipped over to the seat and a broad smile shone all over her face.

"Hello again, somehow I just thought that you might be here", she found herself saying. The normally calm and highly organised Mags was struggling to find words or begin a conversation, and she still could not understand why she felt so strongly that she wanted to talk to him.

"Hello to you too", came the reply, " are you keeping well?"

"I'm fine, can I sit with you for a while, unless I am intruding?"

" Of course you can, I am busy doing nothing again so a little company would be rather nice"

" Look we don't even know each others' names, I'm Mags, well Margaret, really but I much prefer Mags"

" Well hello Mags,nice to meet you, I am Duncan"

The breeze hustled down the open area of the shopping precinct and people passing by turned up collars or clutched coats around them to hold it at bay. In Mags' mind she wanted to suggest heading to the coffee bar for a warm drink but having made such a good start she was concerned that she might frighten him off. That wouldn't be the first time in her life that she had frightened off a possible male friend, in fact she knew she was actually very good at it. The random thoughts, some present, some past, were disturbed by a calm voice that set her pulse racing.

" Last time when we met I did offer you a cup of coffee, and as it is rather chilly today that could be a fair idea". " If you would like to join me for a coffee, then I would be delighted".

"Oh wow, yes please", replied Mags, the excited school girl was returning.

She had not felt like this since a young officer had invited her to the cinema, more years ago than she would wish to own up to. That was a good night, even if his clumsy attempts to hold her hand and put an arm around her ended up more like a silly fumble in the gloom. Well at least he apologised when he realised where his hand had been, even though he was not to know that Mags was not in the least offended. Couldn't tell him that though or he might have wanted more and clumsy he certainly was.

Duncan stood up, offered his hand to Mags to help her from her sitting position to standing. I've met a proper gentleman she thought so he can't have been a police officer, or at least not one of those that she met before.

With coffee cups on a tray they settled into seats in the far corner and began to chatter away as if they had known each other for ages. Mags told him of her career in the force and he listened intently. She explained that she had retired some time before and sometimes found the adjustment to a new life rather trying. Duncan's gentle smile told her that he knew exactly what she was talking about. Without realising it she dominated the conversation, giving Duncan little chance to comment or make any response, but that was typical of Mags, because she had many years of practice in being the leader of all around her. In mid-flow she suddenly stopped, as the realisation that he had not spoken for what seemed like an eternity hit her.

"I'm sorry, here is me going on and on, and you have hardly had a chance to say anything".

"What on earth must you think of me?".

" Well to tell you the truth, I am enjoying just listening as conversation is a bit in short supply in my world".

Duncan, now seizing the initiative, went on to explain that his wife had died some time ago, and although his family and friends had been very supportive there were long periods in his day when his own company was all he had. Mags' brain was shouting, he's single, yes he had to be, and yes there is a sadness about him that I spotted instantly. He told Mags that he had retired some years earlier to look after his wife, as her health deteriorated. Now he simply enjoyed sitting on that seat watching people go by, but he had to admit that he was not sure that he approved of all that he saw. Sign of age was his explanation, but Mags did not feel that he was really that old, indeed being retired all but did not look right. Still he did retire early to look after his wife so perhaps that was it.

Mags could not resist the temptation to take back the initiative and asked about the family that Duncan had mentioned. She looked startled when he pointed out that both of his children were fast approaching fifty, surely not. This look of surprise was noticed by Duncan, who lept in with a quick explanation. We married very young, he explained, after all we met at school and had known each other for a long time by today's standards. The surprise melted from her face at this and Mags just grinned by way of acknowledgment. She was itching to ask what he did as work before he retired . but was determined not to be pushy. Why it mattered so much she was not sure, well not in a way that she could explain to herself.

The coffee cups were empty by this point and they both offered a refill simultaneously. This caused some amusement but Duncan quietly got up, moved to the counter and reappeared with second cups. That voice in Mags' head simply kept repeating, what a nice man. It couldn't be love at first sight but there was a warmth and a connection that she could not deny. They drank their coffee once again in an atmosphere of relaxation and genuine mutual interest.

The girls in the coffee bar were up to their old tricks again and tables were being wiped, coats found and loud goodbyes being said.

"Looks like we had better leave before they throw us out", said Duncan and they both made their way to the door.

"Look" ,announced Mags, " that was most enjoyable we must do it again sometime".

" I was thinking that too, but perhaps I can invite you out for a pub lunch sometime and we can continue our conversation". " My treat because it would be my pleasure".

" That would be rather nice, if I give you my number please call me and we can make arrangements".

An exchange of numbers was swiftly executed and with a brief smile they parted and went their own way. Mags clutched the piece of paper with the telephone number on it and felt herself bounce all the way back to her car. It might be madness, she hardly knew the man, but it just felt right.

Chapter. 13

Mags was so pleased with herself that she could not resist making a quick call to Sara. She rattled off the events of her day, well at least some of them, and told her of the lunch date that was due any minute.

" Well. I can hardly believe it, heavens whatever next ?", Sara breathless said. " hang on a minute Andy is here and I just have to tell him".

" Randy old beggar is what he says, and I have to agree with him".

"Look you can say what you like but it is not like that at all". " He is a nice gentle lonely man and all we are going to do is meet up in a pub for lunch and enjoy a conversation". " The way you two are reacting you would think we were having a bite to eat in the pub, having dessert in bed for the afternoon and then, well, I don't know." "You tell Andy if he mentions condoms I will come round and sort him" .

When the light hearted exchange had reached a conclusion Sara wished Mags well on her date and demanded to know when it was. A long silence followed before the fact that no date had been set was disclosed. Sara could not believe her ears when she was told that he was going to ring her to make arrangements. Deep down she felt that Mags would not wait and it was only a matter of time before Mags made the first move. That would be the Mags that she knew and no dear gentle old chap was likely to change her.

That was an astute observation because it was not long before Mags was prowling around her home glaring at the telephone. She gave it stern looks; she gave it pleading looks; she even made a cup of tea and sat in her chair and pretended to ignore it. Whatever she did the silence from the wretched machine was deafening. She began to wonder if she had written the wrong number down. Perhaps he had lost her scrap of paper with the precious number on it. Typical bloody men, never come up trumps when you want them to, and when they do they have a hundred and one excuses. She wasn't a bad judge of character but perhaps just this once she had got it all wrong.

As she sat there sipping her tea and debating if a biscuit might be a good idea, the telephone burst into life. The cup shot from her hand and she rushed to the phone with her lap awash with tea, giving her an uncomfortable warm feeling that spread through her stomach.

" No I will not answer the bloody questions in your survey, how dare you disturb me, I do not respond to cold calling so go away", she screamed at the defenceless apparatus. Now she had dampness and disappointment in equal measure and needed to sponge herself dry or better still change her skirt. That would have been a simple task but as she was half out of her damp skirt the phone burst into life once again.

"Hello Mags it is Duncan", and her heart skipped a beat.

" Is there a day this week that you would be free for that meal?".

" I can manage any day that suits you",she replied trying not to show the excitement in her voice.

A few moments later and arrangements were set in place. The Golden Lion was a quiet rural pub, with a small restaurant, full of oak beams and character. The date was set for the next day and they agreed to meet in the car park. Duncan sounded pleased that Mags had agreed so readily and Mags, for her part felt much the same.

After the call Mags had forgotten the dampness in her skirt and she threw herself into her chair with a contented purr. She was all too aware that this was all very silly, they hardly knew each other but somehow she felt elated. It had been a long time since she had actually been on a meal date with a man, and so not surprisingly she felt a mixture of apprehension, excitement and perhaps a little shock. What to wear was her next preoccupation, it had to be right, not too dressy but smart and definitely feminine. She stared at her wardrobe and the more she looked the less sure she was about how appropriate each item might be. These feelings were almost alien to her, well they had been for many years, far more than she could remember. She wondered if it was really a date in the real sense or just a meeting of two people who had recently met. Mags tried to calm her racing thoughts but even that did not help.

Chapter 14

Mags tried to call Sara but she was clearly on duty. She sent a brief text to let her know and hoped that at the end of her shift she would pick up any messages. Then she sat and thought that Sara must think she has gone completely mad, charging off with a strange unknown man into the countryside, and probably thought that it was another sign of the advancing years and smacking of desperation. If she had stopped to think she would have known that Sara was not like that. Sara may have had Mags as her boss for only one day but somehow they had formed a bond that would last. She was quite certain that the incident in the antique shop brought them together. After all Sara so wanted it to be a big murder, and Mags had raised hopes about that with her insistence that there was more to it than met the eye. At least Mags was over than nonsense now and seemed to be focussed upon this new man, whoever he was. No real worries there as Mags was famed for being such a good judge of character. If she felt someone was guilty of something she was more often than not proved right even if it did take a bit of hard digging to prove it. Her reputation lived on in the station and ,what would Mags have done, was often a comment during refreshments.

When Sara read the text she immediately replied informing Mags that she would phone for a chat at the end of the shift. Once changed and ready for home she made her call. There was no hurry to get home as Andy would be working into well into the night. This left masses of time for a long natter.

Once she had been given much of the detail Sara could not resist telling Mags how delighted she was for her. If this man was as nice as she said then only good can come from it and who knows what it might lead to. Mags insisted that marriage was not on the menu but a friendship, even a companionship was a big maybe, a bit of a possibility, but by no means a certainty. After all she was really too set in her ways to accommodate radical change in her life. Anyway how can you have a relationship with someone because you originally felt sorry for them for no particular reason.

Sara did agree, but she had already seen a great advantage in what was happening. After all if Mags was so busy with a man in her life then she would stop wondering about that incident and at long last leave it alone. That way everyone will get some peace. After all it was perfectly clear to everyone that in this instance the gut reaction had proved wrong. Sad, but Mags was not infallible, just more right than wrong.

Sara told Mags this and expected to get a reply with all guns blazing. It came as a surprise that a calm Mags quietly agreed with her. Indeed Mags announced that she had hardly given the matter any thought for ages and was happy to accept that there was no deep mystery to be resolved. So she was wrong, well it was not the first time, even if it was a bit on the rare side. As far as she was concerned, the silly old antique bugger keeled over and died, smashing a piece of stock as he fell, the family had a funeral and case closed.

" Tell you what though", Mags found herself saying, " that is a an idea". "Ask Andy will you if anyone attended the funeral quietly". " The Boss would have organised that automatically but the lecherous bastard in charge now probably was too keen to tot up a load of statistics and rub his hands with glee". " Once I have news of how that went, with no surprises or incident then I will officially erase it from my thoughts and he can rest in peace, as can everyone else". "Now that is a fair deal isn't it?".

" I know some of them think I am a daft bitch but barking up trees has long been my speciality".

Reluctantly Sara promised to do as Mags asked, knowing full well that there would be nothing to report, but if it ended the whole sorry mess once and for all it was worth it. Andy was bound to be delighted to help because it was all ancient history, like the old man's stock, and at long last it was not going to be a subject that cropped each time they met.

Sara wished Mags well on her lunch date, hoped for news afterwards and then prepared to hurry home to await the return of Andy. He is going to be so pleased that Mags has finally accepted that the stress of her last day, the trauma of the presentation and all the fuss got in the way of her thinking as clearly as she usually did.

Chapter 15.

Andy laughed when Sara told him of her conversation with Mags. At long last she had accepted that there was nothing in the case and life could carry on without the antique shop nudging its' way into everything. One final piece of information, that was bound to lead to absolutely nowhere, and all would be settled. He already knew the answer to the question because it was he who had be given the task of being present, quietly, at the funeral.

" You can tell her from me, the horses' mouth so to speak, that it was the most uneventful affair I have ever witnessed." " A couple of cars, wife and some family, a few flowers, a short service and everyone left the crematorium as quietly as they had arrived." " The widow shed a few tears, her brother, well I think that was who he was, held her arm and supported her and seemed to be in charge of all that went on." " A small selection of the Chamber of Commerce stood respectfully to the side, a few other odd mourners but that was it." " The only one missing was the daughter, but one of the family friends said that she had moved away years ago and had not kept in touch". "Families, well you know, it happens, so they lost contact so she probably did not know". "Sad but then that sort of thing happens all the time"

Sara breathed a sigh of relief. Not even Mags could make a mountain out of that molehill. She can now concentrate on her mystery man and get on with having good times in her life, and who knows where it might lead. Probably not wedding bells, Not really Mags' style, but a close friendship would be wonderful for her as she tries to grow old gracefully. Mind you with Mags nothing is that simple and she could surprise us all yet.

Her next priority was to pass on the good news to Mags, and hopefully hear all about the lunch date. With the ability of Mags to weave a intricate story that would be well worth listening to, imagination was her strong point and she was so good at telling a tale. Even better when she added bits for effect ,just to see the reaction of her listener.

Chapter 16

On the morning of the lunch date Mags spent more time in front of the mirror than she had ever done. Hair brushed and placed exactly as she wished, a little make-up, but not too much and then she put on the carefully selected clothes. The final inspection made her feel good about herself and she complimented herself upon scrubbing up quite well for an old bird. One last long look in the mirror and it was time to get in the car and drive to the Golden Lion. Mags was an experienced driver and was proud of her record behind the wheel. She had never dented a police car, well not if you don't count reversing into the superintendants car in the yard, but some people thought that was not such an accident as it first appeared. Some history those two but what it was all about they could never find out', and there was no way that Mags was ever going to tell.

Unusual for her, Mags found the wrong gear at the roundabout, causing a motorist behind to use his horn to show his irritation. On any other day Mags would have gone for him in a big way, but she simply smiled a disarming smile and pulled away gently. She knew the road well but found herself carefully looking at every turning so that she did not take an unnecessary detour. This Mags was unsure, even nervous and was so unlike herself that she began to mutter at herself. She was unsure why she was so excited and yet apprehensive, but in a strange way rather liked this alien emotion that flowed through her.

As she pulled into the car park she saw Duncan get out of his car and wave a greeting. She noted in her mind how thoughtful it was of him to ensure that he arrived first. An old fashioned gentlemen who did not keep a lady waiting. Being late was a womans' prerogative. Trying to step calmly and ladylike from her car she managed to get it all wrong. Excitement had caused a memory lapse and she began to get out before undoing the seat belt and so rocked back into her seat instead. Only a warm grin from Duncan saved her from blushing the deepest of red.

" Lovely to see you, Mags",he said and moved swiftly to her side.

" I took the trouble to book a table so we can go in as soon as you like".

" You look very nice if you don't mind my saying so".

"Not at all", a flustered and tongue tied Mags replied.

Mags all shy and nervous, yes she was and she knew it, almost as if a different Mags had come out all dressed up and eager to see him. This wasn't the old Mags, this was a new one and it was a very unnerving feeling, but it had a funny warmth about it that ran from her toes to her ears.

They entered the restaurant area and were quickly shown to their table. Mags could not help but wonder if Duncan had planned this meticulously as they found themselves in a little corner area almost out of sight of everyone. Well privacy was ensured, almost a little love nest just to themselves was the perfect setting.

A read through the menu proved to be a distraction from these thoughts careering through her mind, like autumn leaves caught up in a high wind that swirled them around completely out of control. A drinks order and food confirmed they settled down and began what was to be a long conversation in hushed tones. Duncan paid her another compliment on how she looked, carefully adding that she always had looked smart when they met previously. Mags too had noticed how well dressed Duncan was, slightly casual but smart nevertheless. Spot on for a lunch date but not over the top as a dinner date might be.

The conversation began, after a few pleasantries, with Duncan asking how Mags was adjusting to retirement. Having been down that road himself he had an understanding of how the changes can affect everyday life. He hoped to hear more about her time in the force as he felt sure there were lots of funny tales to be told.

Mags didn't feel it was such a good idea to tell some of the tales, they might not be too well received. You can't tell a relative stranger that you had kneed a colleague in the groin for making a pass at you. Nor can you tell how you thought of those around you a friends, colleagues and bastard, especially her many battles with the bastards.

Instead she spoke very generally about the good times, friendships, cold night patrols, the joy of a warm car on a frosty night and the silly antics of drunken revellers on a Saturday night. Not surprisingly she did not feel it appropriate to tell of the incident in the pub when she poured beer down the inside of someones' trousers.

The food and drinks arrived as Mags was warming to some of her tales, which gave her a chance to pause in mid flow. She was about to kick off again between mouthfuls, when Duncan rocked her back in her seat with a question.

"What is the real difference between murder and manslaughter?", he asked in a matter of fact way," only explain it in simple terms because I don't understand all that legal jargon".

A few seconds dragged by and Mags was glad she had a mouthful of food so that she was unable to respond immediately. Her mind was chasing around trying to make sense of such an unusal thing to ask over a meal in a pub.

"Well, that is a surprising question but the answer is a bit like, murder is unlawful killing usually with plans before the crime so to speak, whereas manslaughter is a death caused sometimes by accident or lack of care".

"Does that make sense to you?"

" Yes, fine, so manslaughter could be someone dying even if that was not quite what you intended?"

" Where is this leading?", asked Mags .

"Nowhere, just something I have often wondered about and I have never had the chance to ask someone who would know". " Sorry that was a conversation stopper and I did not mean to do that at all"

" No problem, never mind, I was going to tell you some more about me but I honestly would prefer to hear a little about you".

" After all I know almost nothing and I am sitting here enjoying a nice meal and a chat with you".

" Well there is not a great deal to tell, I specialise in being ordinary, but at least you know I am on my own now"

Duncan went on to tell Mags about his work, a little about his family but offered very little detail. Even a little gentle coaxing from Mags did not get him to release information about what he actually did. The responses were almost disarming as he would jokingly point out that his work was routine and very ordinary unlike hers which was full of excitement.

When the conversation turned to his wife, Duncan became much quieter and Mags was worried that she had touched a raw nerve. Being Mags she just had to say what she felt and was stunned by the response that came from Duncan. He assured her that he had come to terms with his grief but one issue still haunted him. The two of them had a wonderful relationship all the years they were together and shared and told each other everything. He went on to explain that on only one occasion had he kept something from her for fear of hurting her feelings, and had decided eventually to tell her only to find she went into a coma from which she never recovered. His sadness was that she was never told the truth, was unable to reassure me that she understood, did not get the opportunity let me know how she felt.

"Good Lord, what on earth did you not tell her?, Mags blurted out without thinking. She then cringed inside at such an insensitive remark.

"Forgive me, but it very personal and very , well you know, and perhaps when I have known you for a year or so I might be able to tell you". Don't be offended because none of the family know, in fact absolutely nobody knows so you are in good company".

He quickly retrieved a difficult situation by suggesting that they came out for a meal together and serious conversation can get in the way of having an enjoyable time. Mags smiled an understanding smile, secretly cursing herself for her insensitivity. She dived back into her police repertoire and mentioned that on her final day she thought that her colleagues were playing tricks on her, but gave no detail or information about the who, the what and the where. The police officer in here was far too strong to pass on information to the public. Duncan smiled at this and, almost as if by magic, asked about her retirement do, speeches and simply having to stand there and be embarrassed. Mags was on safe ground once again and was soon into a blow by blow account of the events of that evening especially how she got in a few low blows on the bastards in the attic.

They were still laughing when they were asked if they wanted a dessert and after some deliberation decided to share one, which duly arrived with two spoons and a grin from the waitress. As they tucked in they just smiled at one another, Duncan feeling that a difficult moment had passed and Mags so glad that she had not put her foot in it completely.

Over coffee, Duncan asked Mags if she would care to meet up again, and her heart did its' little trick of missing a mini-beat. She noticed that Duncan's hand was flat on the table and reached across and held it as she declared how much she would enjoy such a prospect. They made their way to their cars smiling and chatting away and, having chorused that they would each phone the other, they went their separate ways. This time Mags put her concentration on to the road and the other traffic and had an uneventful journey home. Uneventful except for a strange feeling moving all over her. This was an experience she had not felt for a very long time, an experience that allowed an arm of comforting hug surround her, the sort of glow that has no explanation but was nevertheless real and pleasing.

Chapter 17

When Sara phoned, later that evening, Mags could not help but notice the excitement and anticipation in her voice. There were enough clues in her voice to suggest that there would be a lot of fun in exaggerating a few things, in adding the odd bits, just to tease her a little. The very thought tickled Mags' mind as she began her conversation. Well young Sara if you want me to tell you all, then I shall, but with a few extras, not lies, just push the boundaries a bit, so Mags eased into her report on the date. She began her report with a deep sigh and a great apology for shocking Sara. A good start that, because it is bound to grab the attention and hold it for absolutely ages.

She told Sara that she was unsure what she must think of her. After all they sat in a quiet secluded area away from prying eyes and held hands. The meal was really good but the company was even better. The conversation flowed non-stop with lots of laughter and smiles, never a dull moment with her new man. They chatted away about each other, he listening to tales of her career and he in turn sharing with her moments from his life. The chemistry between them was electric and they couldn't wait to arrange another date as soon as possible. This next time Mags thought that she could cook a meal at her home and that might lead to a cuddle on the settee.

All the time Sara simply made sounds of "oh" and "wow", which only made Mags push those boundaries even further. Pushing those boundaries to the point where she might come to regret it. She was having fun and she did not care!

Over coffee he told me of some of his deepest thoughts and it was very touching. He just opened up his heart and the words tumbled out. It was so wonderful to share personal secrets with someone like that. It was as if we had known each other for ages and ages and were so relaxed and happy in each others' company. We both agreed it was the best date we had for a million years, well at least as far back as when Black Forest Gateau was top of the dessert list on the menu. Sara continued to listen in awe and uttered a deep gasp, when she was told that they shared a dessert together like a young couple starting out. Mags pointed out that in younger days, sharing a dessert like that was the first step towards sharing a bed. Not like the modern youngsters who cut out all the preliminaries and just dive on each other without giving the consequences a thought. That's why there are so many unmarried mothers about, not enough sharing of a Black Forest gateau or any other bloody sweet for that matter.

"Ruddy hell Mags", was all Sara could say, but it was enough to pull Mags back from any further plunging into the depths of her imagination." I suppose you actually know his name now, that might be handy before you roll about all over your settee"" It was months before I let Andy touch me at all, so don't think for a moment that all youngsters are at it from day one".

" I didn't mean you love", Mags quickly threw into the conversation, " you know what I mean, not you, all those other buggers that I am now paying for!"

" Well you hit it off well, great, but what is his name, what else is there to tell?".

"He is called Duncan, he is smart, interesting and a delight to be with".

" One word to anyone, other than Andy of course, and I will come looking for you, and the revenge of Mags is to be feared I promise you".

"Now you know I would not drop you in it, I promised and I will keep my word".

" Oh I nearly forgot, did Andy discover anything about the funeral that is worth knowing?".

Sara relayed the news just as Andy had told her.

Mags' reaction was encouraging to Sara because she simply accepted the limited detail and even joked that the missing daughter was not too much of a surprise because if she had a daughter she would have left home at an early age, probably pushing herself along in her pushchair. The two of them giggled at the thought of a baby of Mags, would have left home before it could even walk. Maternal and Mags were not two words that were likely to appear in the same sentence.

Chapter 18.

Duncan sat in his favourite armchair and allowed his mind to reflect on the events of the day. Mags was a really delightful character, strong and forceful, yes, but there was a softer almost vulnerable side to her too. He doubted if many people ever got to see that or even sense that it was there. The meal had been a success and there was another chance to meet in the offing. Taking his hand like that was a bit of a surprise, but a nice one, and it actually felt right, so being surprised rather puzzled him. He grinned as he recalled some of her police exploits. All in all it was a good lunchtime meeting and clearly there was a mutual wish to meet up again soon. It is all very well saying that you will phone but when is the appropriate time he wondered. If you make an immediate call you might be seen as too keen or anxious, if you leave it too late and indifference comes into play. He came to the conclusion that you just pick a convenient moment and hope you get it right. He did wonder about arranging for some flowers, but the concern that it might be seen as pushy held him back and he decided to hold on to that idea until after another meeting or two. She was a lovely lady, a good companion and deserved to be treated with respect.

He reached for the phone and dialled the number but found that it was engaged. Well a lady like that must have a circle of friends so the call will have to wait. He smiled at the photo of Helen on the side table by his arm and spoke to it as if she was still in the room with him. Just a few details of his meeting with Mags,were said, perhaps seeking reassurance that she would approve of him moving on with his life. He knew deep down that she would as she had told him enough times that it was what he ought to do.

He reached for the phone again, pressed redial, and found himself thrilled that the ringing tone sprung into life. Mags answered almost at the first ring, she could hardly have moved more than a few inches since her call with Sara. Duncan thanked her for such a pleasant time and was relieved to hear that Mags felt much the same. She even suggested there and then that next time he might like to come to her home and she would cook a meal. Duncan protested that he did not wish to add work for her and he would be more than happy for them to go out to eat once again, although he felt sure she was a very good cook. Mags chuckled aloud at this and pointed out that her preparing a meal for someone was a rare thing but those who had eaten her food, did not complain, were still alive so she had not managed the perfect murder yet.

Duncan offered to contact her just before the weekend and added as an afterthought unless they met up on the seat in the shopping arcade before then. Mags was not sure if this was an invite or not.

When Mags tried to apologise for asking questions that were too personal during the meal, Duncan reassured her that he was not offended at all. Indeed he hoped that he had not cut her short rudely by what he had said, or rather what he did not say. They wished each other a restful night and the call ended.

Duncan looked long and hard at the photo. In his head he could hear a familiar voice telling him that she understood. No, she had not realised what he had done but to her he would always be her hero, her protector the one person she could always turn to. She was proud of him nothing would ever change that......

The voice faded away and Duncan's eyes closed as he sat back and rested in his armchair. His conscious mind was at rest but somewhere his subconscious was still taking thoughts on a journey.

Chapter 19

Duncan's mind turned to those distant days of his teenage years and the times he spent with Helen. He vividly remembered the things she said of her early childhood and how his arm encircled her protectively. The returning of the arm when he removed it was a moment he could never forget. Nor could he forget the shock he felt when she told him one part of her story.

Just before her ninth birthday, she was alone at home when a visitor called. Her father was on the afternoon shift so he would not be home until after the pub shut. Her mother had gone out shopping and was not expected back until it was time for making a snack for tea. She hurried to the door to find the landlord of the pub standing there with his daughter, little Victoria who was a year or so younger than Helen.

Discovering that mother was out he invited themselves in to wait for her return as there was a message about a pub event he wanted to share with her. To pass the time the two girls chatted merrily and when he suggested they read a story everyone piled onto the settee, he in the middle with one on each side. Helen had found a story book and he picked it up and began to read. Having a story read was much better than just sitting all alone watching the clock go round. She could not recall how the two girls came to be holding opposite sides of the book as he read, but that is how the story session continued. Helen noticed that her father had placed his hand on Victoria's knee and then realised that his other hand was on hers. As the story progressed the hand moved around her knee and from time to time moved along her leg. It seemed strange but Victoria was sitting still listening to the story with little expression on her face so she thought little more about it.

Some time passed and the story had reached an exciting part when Victoria's father announced that the pub was soon to open. He told Victoria that she should run down to her mother, tell her he was delayed and would be there shortly, once the message was delivered to Helen's mother. She was told to stay there as it would be time for her meal before the pub became busy. Victoria stood up, and without speaking, went to the front door and left as instructed.

The story continued with Helen holding the book as before. Victoria's father suggested that she would be more comfortable on his lap so that she could follow the words and look at the pictures as he read. He eased her gently on to his lap and continued to read. The hand returned to her knee and from time to time made an excursion upwards along her leg. Helen found this odd but made no comment or made any reaction. Well into the story, Helen became aware that the hand had left her leg and was now moving very slowly across her stomach. When she moved a little, she was told she was alright and felt she should sit still as she had been told. She began to freeze as the hand moved her underwear aside and began to touch her body. This was like nothing she had ever known before and she felt unable to move or respond in any way. No words came into her mouth and she was unable to make any sounds. The hand continued to move around and she was aware that the flat of the hand was now more like a finger moving firmly at her.

Some instinct forced her to jump up dropping the book and just staring at the man grinning at her. He got to his feet and she felt very scared. He turned towards the door and told her he would return later when mother was at home to deliver the message. As he reached the door he turned to Helen and told her that she should not tell anyone about their"fun", but at any time if she wanted some sweets or a bit of pocket money she had only let him know and he would make sure she was provided with whatever she wanted. As he left through the door she was stunned with his voice telling her that for a little more "fun" she could have whatever she wanted anytime. She may well have fancied some sweets or a little pocket money but not if she had to put up with his finger doing things to her.

When her mother returned she blurted out briefly that the landlord had been with a message but had left to return later. When she also added that he had put his hand up her skirt whilst reading a story, her mother told her she was making it up and it was never to be mentioned again. When her mother added that Dad would not be able to use that pub again she felt positively sick.

A few days later she did mention it to Victoria, who shrugged her shoulders, sighed and said nothing.

The incident was never spoken of again until that evening as she and Duncan sat together and she told him. That arm must have been the first comfort she had received since that dreadful day years before. Duncan's reaction was to attack the man, his pub and anyone who got in his way, but he also knew he would not be strong enough to inflict the kind of damage he had in mind. Whilst he held, Helen his mind began to formulate plans on how revenge or justice could be handed down. Helen for her part just wanted it to all go away, she no longer had bad dreams about it, and certainly could not face any public fuss. Duncan knew he was helpless in terms of dealing with it for her, but he knew that just being at her side, caring for her and being gentle was all that she really needed. Neither girl was prepared to face the world about the events, but maybe one day, justice can be delivered.

Chapter 20

Mags waited until the morning had fully broken but could contain herself no longer. She just had to phone Duncan. She wanted to entertain him in her home, where they could talk and share experiences in comfort and seclusion. The invite had to be made and she felt the need to take the initiative.

" Good morning Duncan, Mags here, thought I would just call and see if you would care to come over to my place for a bite to eat later today or perhaps tomorrow".

" Well that would be nice but I need to go into town this morning as there are a couple of things I need to do". " I could pop over and see you after that if you wish, but it might be helpful if I knew where you lived!"

Mags laughed out loud at this and quickly gave directions. Duncan assured her that he knew the way and that he hoped to be there by midday.

People who knew Mags would never have described her movement as skipping, but by the end of the call she was skipping around the house getting ready for her visitor. This new, changed, Mags was a different person to the old one, lighter in step, broader in smiles and with a zest for life. Even Mags was beginning to see how her whole world was changing, and for the better. As she organised some food she kept glancing at the clock, glaring at the way it refused to speed up, and kept an ear to the door bell that simply would not ring. She knew there was an hour to go, but he might, just might, be early!

As she flicked at her hair and straightened her blouse she looked at the mirror, which did not answer her as she spoke to the image she could see in it.

" Bloody hell Mags, what is happening to you girl, you've gone back to being a teenager!"

Chapter 21

Mags could still run if she had to but when the doorbell finally rang she, literally, sprinted to the door. Standing there was Duncan with a bunch of flowers and a broad smile. She reached forward to greet him and gave him a gentle kiss on the cheek. She ushered him into the house and close the door behind them.

After the preliminaries of greetings had finished, she organised a coffee and they sat in the two armchairs and just smiled at each other. Mags explained that she had arranged a light lunch and hope that Duncan would enjoy it. They chatted for a while and then Mags moved them both to the dining table and they sat down to enjoy their meal. As ever ,Duncan, the gentleman, complimented Mags on the food and tucked in merrily.

As they ate they talked about no particular matter, just general chat, and seemed to be perfectly relaxed and at ease with each other.

" Look Mags, I am sorry I was a bit abrupt over our pub lunch when you asked about what I regret I had not told my wife" " That was a little rude of me but my excuse is that the question was a bit of a surprise and caught me on the wrong foot".

" No it was my rudeness I should have known better, it is me who should apologise".

" Don't be silly, no apology necessary, and anyway you deserve an answer". " Years ago as a young child my wife was sexually assaulted by the local pub landlord, who was clearly doing the same or worse to his own daughter". " At the time I found out, I was still at school and could not see a way to sort it out as she wanted desperately to leave the past in the past". " God how I wanted to fix him once and for all"." His own daughter as well, you can't get lower than that".

At this Mags lept to her feet rushed to his side and kissed him full on the mouth. Duncan looked shocked but in less than a second the explanation came flying.

" A daughter, a bloody daughter, of course, not at the funeral, no surprise, that's the answer, you've come up with the answer Duncan, genius, bloody genius!".

As Mags slumped back into her chair and Duncan looked at her with astonishment written all over his face, she began to explain herself.

She reminded him of how on her final day she thought her colleagues were playing tricks with a fake murder. Well, she went on to explain, deep down she knew there was something not quite right about it and he, Duncan, had come up with the answer. Not the same but similar and at last she was on the trail of a possible solution.

As Duncan still looked in a state of shock and had not spoken or made any attempt to reply Mags rushed in with an apology for the kiss, hoping that he would understand that her excitement had taken over. For ages she had struggled to make sense of something and then bang enlightenment.

Duncan calmly suggested that they change the subject as it was rather too close to home for him and being arrested for murder by his lunch date was not part of his plans for the day. Mags roared with laughter at this, he had such a dry sense of humour it fascinated her, but she wasted no time in agreeing. The rest of the afternoon could be ruined if old wounds were opened and his sensitivity was one of the things that attracted her.

The conversation turned to a range of other things including her garden, which resembled a mini jungle. Since she had retired she had promised herself that she would get out there and really tidy it up, but with one thing and another, she always found and excuse to leave it for another day.

" Too busy having meals with strange men", suggested Duncan, " still it is only a small patch and won't take long once you get down to it".

The conversation moved on to Duncan's garden and he too found that it was not getting the attention it deserved. Doing nothing is a time consuming occupation, which leaves little room for other things. Mags noticed that her clock, after behaving so badly earlier on, was now racing round at an alarming rate. She made a mental note to check the batteries because she was unsure if clocks went faster or slower as the batteries became run down . Whichever it was, this clock clearly had a mind of its own and was doing its best to annoy her. Someone once said time flies when you are having fun, but it is not time, it is clocks, who wait until you are enjoying yourself and then turn on the envy and muck it all up. If someone could invent a clock that did not become jealous of the owner having a good time, they would make a fortune.

The clock was winning the battle because Duncan announced that he ought to be leaving to allow Mags to enjoy the rest of her day.

" No need to rush off if you don't need to, stay the night if you like, oh no, I meant stay for some of the evening, night ,whatever". " Look that came out all wrong, I am not doing anything in particular if you care to stay a bit longer".

" It is a lovely offer, but honestly, I have promised to phone my daughter early this evening and that can usually be a long call". " Quite why she thinks I need checking on so frequently is beyond me, but if she phones me and I am not there she can start to go frantic".

Mags desperately wanted to know when they might meet up again and quickly made arrangements to meet up for coffee in a couple of days at the coffee bar. Duncan readily agreed and so she felt that at least she had not frightened him off. Kissing him like that is one thing , but inviting him to stay the night was pushing it a bit far. Deep down, however, she was not sure that she would have minded if he had accepted the offer as it stood.

She stood framed in the doorway and waved him goodbye, watching the car disappear into the distance and around the corner. A strange sense of loss eased across her and she felt puzzled that she was missing him already. Half a minute is hardly time to miss anyone but miss him she did.

Chapter 22.

The next telephone call to Sara was extremely brief.

" Sara, get yourself round here as soon as you are able I have some startling news".

" Ok Mags ,but what is going on?"

"Never mind that I need to see you"

Sara threw on her coat and set off in her car towards Mags' home. Her mind was all over the place, something had happened, but the urgency in her voice suggested that Mags was excited not concerned. She parked at the kerbside and ran to the front door which swung open as she reached it.

"Come in , come in, I've made the coffee"

" Slow down Mags for goodness sake you've got me worried"

" Look I am in love, well not exactly but you will see what I mean". " I kissed him full on the lips, then I asked him to stay the night, he just got me so excited".

"He's not upstairs in bed still is he?"

" Don't be so stupid but I have masses to tell you, and you are not going to believe what I have to say".

When the whirlwind of words reached a gentle breeze Sara began to take in some of what Mags had to say. So they were getting along famously and he mentioned something that triggered that dramatic response, a dramatic response in terms of a full kiss. Sara listened as she was told of a friendly meal, when Duncan mentioned something from years ago that had fired the thought processes of Mags. The daughter was the missing clue, the daughter who did not turn up for her father's funeral, the same one who left home at an early age and never made contact again. The whole thing centred around the daughter.

Sara still felt that this was a great leap in the dark, but there were suggestions of logic, hints of sense and a distinct lack of Mags and her imagination running riot once again. They discussed the possibility of the father being the cause of the flight of the daughter, logical if he was having sex with her. The issue of mother and if she had an awareness raised itself too.

" The bloody daughter did for him, but how I am not sure".

" Yes I can see where you are heading, the shock of seeing her after all these years would be enough to give him a heart attack, especially if she was now going expose him for what he was".

"Well he would not be flavour of the month in the Chamber of Commerce when they found out would he?"

"That could explain the sudden withdrawl from the council elections too".

" Christ Mags you have opened up a whole new line of enquiry".

" Yes, maybe, but we need to think about this carefully, it is a minefield of problems". " How do we prove any of what is only a theory?" " Can' t see the wife telling all, if she knew, as she will have seen the past buried with him". " If other youngsters were involved it is strange that we did not have a whisper or a small complaint from ages ago". " The key would be to find this girl, but we don't know her name, anything about her or any clue as to where she might be". " Told you, staggering news but also a massive problem".

The two of them sat and fired ideas, possibilities at each other and with each one the final resolution seemed to move further away. It made sense, it was logical, but proof was elusive. No witnesses, no clues about the daughter, just an idea about the old man was not a lot to go on. They paused in silence for a few moments each searching the innermost recesses of their minds to find a way forward.

Mags broke the silence with a remark that only Mags could have made.

"The way I see it is, that although it would be good to tie it all up, if we are right, the old bugger got what he deserved so maybe it should be left alone, except that the poor girl clearly needs help as she must have been unable to cope with the past". " There is not much chance of bringing him to court because judges don't like trying corpses, even less so when they have been cremated, although a small urn would take up less room than a coffin".

Chapter 23

When she received a phone call telling her that her old boss, the superintendant, wanted to see her, Mags was sure that this was where she was told formally to back off from any further private snooping. With an appointment made, she arrived at the station in good time, having parked in the public car park a hundred yards away. No privilege of parking for her, she was one of the public not one of them. As she walked up to the main doors from the street she noticed a few familiar faces looking down from windows above. A few paces took her through the foyer and she was facing the reception desk. No need for introductions because an old friend stood there smiling at her.

"Welcome back sarge, you look good, retirement must suit you, The Boss is expecting you I will get someone to take you upstairs,".

A young officer appeared from nowhere and ushered her forward and up to the Superintendant's office. He knocked on the door and at the shout of "enter", Mags was shown inside. Sitting at his desk was The Boss, her dear friend, but he was not looking severe as she had expected, there was a wide smile that split his face.

"Wonderful to see you Mags, take a seat"

As she sat a further knock at the door heralded further arrivals and Sara and Andy marched in, responded to the nod from The Boss and also sat down.

"Right, before you go leaping off at the deep end, this is a thank you meeting and one between old friends." " It is informal because it has to be and let me make it clear that both Andy and Sara are true loyal friends and exactly what you trained them to be, professional". " No testicles are to be removed, crushed or anything, your old days are over mores the pity".

The Boss winked at her as he said this and Mags began to relax. The Boss told how the two young officers had come to him in confidence and that he appreciated their actions. Yes he did know of the new man in her life and he was delighted for her. Andy and Sara had noticed a new spring in her step and it obviously suited her. All that is a private matter and it was to stay that way, but if a wedding appeared on the horizon he expected to be invited to be the best man. He joked that he had been trying to give her away for years and the little group laughed at his remark.

" Now, business, Mags, I want to help but am tied by rules and stuff as you know".

"It would be more than bad form to over –rule a colleague, unless I can prove he is totally wrong".

" You always said that a vital clue was hidden somewhere, and good heavens it looks as if you were right and have unearthed it"

"This daughter idea makes a lot of sense, but the case is officially close and I cannot reopen it without cast iron new evidence, which CID will not put themselves out to find".

"You of all people know how it works so this needs some subtle handling and a great deal of tact and experience".

The Boss went on to outline his strategy that might help to clarify the whole matter. He appreciated that to put one over on the bastards on the top floor would be the crowning moment since her retirement. He had arranged for Andy to be on a special secondment for one day a week attached to his office, and Sara was more than willing to be the liaison link between her and the centre of things. Not a single soul in the station was aware of what was happening and that was the way it was to stay. As far as everyone was concerned he had invited Mags in to see him as part of his overall pastoral role at the station, particularly for retired officers, a new idea he had thought up, which pleased the politically correct brigade and actually made sense anyway. So the only question was where did Mags fit into the scheme of things, because she was no longer authorised to be formally involved.

Andy took over the conversation, pointing out that he had access to all the current information and he would be talking to Mags about it and hoping to get her professional input. Confidentiality was critical and the strictest professionalism was not only expected but everyone knew it would be delivered.

"Right", he began opening a pile of folders that he had with him," the daughter is called Victoria, although even that may be changed by now". " There has been no trace of her since she left, almost forty years ago so it has to be born in mind that she is about retirement age and having disappeared that deep is going to be all but impossible to trace. There is no national insurance trace, no pension record in her original name, so she has either changed her identity completely or she might even be dead.

Mags winced at this thought because that one had not occurred to her. However if the daughter confronted her father then she is alive, or someone did it on her behalf.

Andy told Mags that he had researched background as far back as 30 years when Reginald Morris bought and moved into the antique shop. He was trying to get back before then but had drawn a blank as probably the wife is the only one who can supply the information, and alerting her would be risky just in case she has a knowledge of what it is all about, perhaps even being directly involved. As any information came to light Sara would relay it, and Mags it was hoped would chew it over and make suggestions and prod lines to follow.

Mags, still slightly stunned, nodded her agreement and looked at the beaming face of The Boss sitting in front of her. He still had the air of a handsome and fit male, just a little older than when she had seen him in the shower in her flat all those years ago. The uniform just made him look even more distinguished and anyway his wife had the pleasure of that body now, lucky girl.

The Boss concluded their meeting by returning to hear about the new man, this Duncan, who had swept her off her feet. Mags finally fell for a man, kissing him on a first date, holding hands and even inviting him to spend the night. The Boss was laughing as he said this and Mags felt herself blush.

"Lovely to see you my dear, take care and if you run out of my little gift to you, give me a call and I will rush fresh supplies round by squad car!"

Chapter 24

As she left the station to return to her car Mags felt elated. If Andy could track someone down, or get to the bottom of it all, he could and she would have the pleasure of quietly helping him in the background. Sara had walked with her and Mags smiles at the thought of getting a police escort back to her car. She liked the idea of the public seeing this and drawing conclusions that would be wide of the mark. It fitted her sense of fun perfectly.

She sat in her car for a while and reflected on what she had been told. The girl left years ago, almost as soon as they moved into the shop. Well hidden but there must be someone out there who has a little bit of background and she rather fancied her chances of finding that someone and putting the jigsaw together. When you do a jigsaw you usually start with the straight edges, and then slowly build up the whole picture. Now the shape and the picture was beginning to show itself. She tried hard to resist it but she could not help thinking that Mags was infallible after all.

At home she sat and stared at the wall her mind moving around in its' own mysterious way. Thoughts of how she could dig out a few more facts spun and danced in her brain even though she fought hard to remember that professionalism was the key word and she had no authorisation. That had not stopped her in the past but this time she had to be very careful. If she made a mistake, one small slip and she would place the Boss in a dreadful position and she would never do that.

Bless you Duncan, she thought, one little chance remark and you have got everything rolling once again. She was unsure if she believed in a divine organiser, fate, or whatever it might be called but there must be something. This fate, or whatever, had drawn her to the elderly man on the seat. That was difficult to explain. It must have pushed her into a conversation, urged her on to coffee, then on to meals and all to guide her to the ultimate solution of the events of her final day. In addition to all this guidance fate had brought her to a really gentle and kind man, a warm friend and companion to share her later years. Thanks fate you are a star, I owe you one!

Chapter 25

Mags was itching to phone Duncan to tell him her news, but of course she knew that would be wrong, discretion was the key or the whole matter could grind to a shuddering halt. Still, she had a lot to occupy her thoughts, her new man and the possibility of confounding everyone and solving events at the antique shop. The first of these thoughts was soon kicked into action when Duncan phoned in the evening. It was nice to hear his voice but despite wishing to tell him all her news she knew that the confidentiality was essential. She listened as Duncan explained that he had an appointment at the optician the next morning and he hoped that Mags might be free to join him for coffee when he had finished. He joked that it seemed only yesterday that he had his sight tested and yet it was actually two years.

" Time flies when you are enjoying yourself, so you must have had plenty to keep your mind busy", remarked Mags.

" Well it certainly has flown since I met you"

Mags felt herself blush, but the words made her feel, in a strange way, special.

They agreed to meet at midday in the usual place, at the coffee bar, and Duncan chuckled as he reminded her that being earlier in the day they might not get thrown out by the staff this time.

With arrangements for the next day set in place, Mags returned to the other main feature of her current world. She need an excuse to go into the antique shop, after all she was unlikely to be recognised because she had hardly met any of the people involved, that was left to Andy and the others. She wondered if she got inside and struck up a conversation, someone might just mention something that would lead her forward. The daughter was the key but you can't just march in and ask where the missing daughter is. She then realised that, as her meeting with Duncan would not be until lunchtime, she could easily wander in off the street during the morning, look around and see if anyone would engage in a gentle conversation. In her mind she practised a range of remarks and comments that might get things going but she more she thought the more contrived her ideas became. They would see it coming and clam up immediately. She came to the conclusion that it was probably best just to wander in, look at a few items and wait and see what develops.

Mags decided that she ought to dress up for this visit in the smartest outfit she could find in her wardrobe. After all it was important that she looked as if she could afford to buy antiques and she had seen some of the price tags. She knew nothing much about pots and glass and all that stuff but perhaps looking for a piece of jewellery was a safer bet. Rings, broaches and necklaces were at least things she felt comfortable with and are the sort of thing you can spend ages looking, wondering about and then getting into conversation.

It did occur to her that perhaps she ought to inform Andy what she was thinking, but then if she did he might just veto it. Even worse he may suggest that she has a companion, witness, and with her and then send out some tired old devil who would get in the way. No they couldn't do that because the people in the know where limited and very exclusive. Heaven forbid he would suggest that she take Duncan. No that was not on, he had already done enough and there was no reason to drag him into anything. He may have provided a spark, but it had absolutely nothing to do with it and it would be unfair to get him involved. She secretly thought that he might be very good at keeping a conversation going in the shop, and a good excuse for not buying anything if the price was high, but involvement was not an option. She resolved to keep him out of it, he was her private life and this matter was something completely different.

Satisfied that this was the right way forward she settled into her chair. Although she had switched on the television she was not really taking much notice of the programme and began to doze and drift off to sleep. She woke with a start when the programme changed and the following one had loud introductory music.

" I swear they put up the sound for the adverts", she announced to herself and made preparations to head off to bed.

Chapter 26

In the morning Mags, dressed in the smart outfit she had chosen, with hair brushed and neatly in place, set off for the short journey into the town. With the care safely parked in the usual car park she set off towards the shops. As she left the precinct she could not help herself as she glanced back at the seat, and as expected it was empty. She turned the corner and went on along the High Street. Turning left at the traffic lights she came to a quiet road with a few shops, a selection of charity shops, an estate agents and finally the antique shop. She paused outside to compose herself and busied herself window shopping. She could see an arrangement of pottery, some wooden ornaments and a small case with pieces of jewellery. A Victoria pendant caught her eye and she decided that this would be an ideal item to open a conversation.

As she entered the shop she looked deliberately at the counter and the floor around it. This time of course there was no body lying there or evidence that there had ever been one. She moved towards the counter a lady appeared from a back room. This lady of retirement age was wearing a tabard and was carrying a duster.

"I would like to have a look at the Victorian pendant in the window please", announced Mags.

" Certainly madam, I will get it out for you to look at more closely". "Rather a nice piece and very old, but ideal for that special occasion". " Are you attending a function or is it a gift?".

" Neither really, I just saw it in the window and thought how delicate it looked".

"Well I can't tell you much about it because I don't really work in the shop, I am just keeping an eye on things whilst Mrs. Morris is out with a friend". I am her cleaner and help out when she is busy". "I've worked for her for years since before they moved here".

Mags could spot an opening, and this was laid on a plate so she pressed on swiftly.

" Has that been a long time then?"

" Well, when they moved here from London I was given the job looking after the house and the shop and that was over twenty years ago".

" Did they have a large antique shop in London then, Mr. Morris must be a bit of an expert".

"Mr. Morris is no longer here, he died a while back, ever so sad and it means I have a lot more to do, but I don't mind because I lost my husband several years ago so it helps to keep me busy". " Mrs.Morris is alright though because she has Mr. Gregory to keep her company".

"Mr. Gregory, is that her brother?"

"No dear she doesn't have a brother, he is a sort of boyfriend, if you can have a boyfriend at their age". " He has been around for ages, long before Mr. Morris died, some people think they were together even in London and he moved here to be with her". " Oh dear you must think that I am an awful gossip and you came here to look at the pendant, here it is, lovely isn't it?"

" It certainly is but it looks as if it is out of my price range, but I am sure that there are others that you might be able to show me"." Must have been hard for Mrs. Morris losing her husband suddenly like that, and with no family to support her".

" Well there is a daughter but she left home years ago, just before they left here to run the pub in London". " She is never mentioned so I never ask about it".

" Run a pub, but I thought Mr. Morris was an antiques expert".

" Look these two pendants are rather nice and less expensive too". " Goodness me no, he knew a lot about antiques but he was actually a publican". "Left the Vale Estate on the other side of town years ago to run the London one then came back and opened up here".

" Oh, I do like the amethyst one, that would look wonderful on a dress that I have in mind to wear". " At twenty pounds that is quite reasonable". "I ought to ask my partner though before I spend all his money, although I am sure he will agree".

" Gentlemen, should always splash out on their ladies I always say, Mr. Gregory gives Mrs. Morris all sorts of beautiful things, which is lovely at their time of life".

By now Mag's brain was racing and she needed to take steady breaths to ensure that her excitement did not show. He ran a pub, daughter left, they moved , now back. It is beginning to fall into place. She wondered what risks were involved in attempting to engage Mrs.Morris in conversation at a later date. The key question was if anyone had a clue as to where the daughter was.

" I think I will talk to my partner, I am meeting him at lunchtime, so I might be able to call back later". "Must be sad to lose contact with a daughter like that, especially as there has been no word since".

" Oh yes, if I lost touch with mine I would be devastated." " Mind you someone told me that the daughter and the father had a big bust up, but kids are like that, I was lucky with my Victoria, she was a good child and never any trouble". " The Morris's Victoria was obviously a different kettle of fish altogether".

At this Mags knew she had to get out of the shop. Thoughts were not just flying around in her brain they were dive bombing it.

" Well look, you have been ever so helpful, I am extremely grateful, and hopefully I can call back later to get the pendant".

" We are open till five today so anytime will be fine dear".

Mags made for the door and drew deep breaths of the fresh cool air. She walked briskly back towards the main shops. Making contact with Sara was now a priority, but one thought was holding her back. " Coincidence is one thing, chance, well not really, the inescapable fact was that it was more than likely that her dear Duncan knew more about this than he mentioned. If so why did he only give sketchy detail, was the thought that pushed itself to the front of her thinking.

She sat on the seat by the coffee bar and stared into empty space.

Chapter 27.

" Hello stranger, fancy seeing you here", a familiar voice said as Mags sat in silence unaware of anything around her".

She turned slowly to see Sara standing there.

" Hello, Sara I did not see you there, must have been miles away, deep in thought".

"I am on my way to the car park, idiot teenagers causing trouble again, two of us are going in from the road and I am going to block the lifts". " At least it is not that clown you tipped us off about, he is doing community service in the park, but I gather he is hopeless, no real surprise he had as much brain as a small insect".

"Look I need to talk to you later, give me a call when you are finished for the day, it is important".

"As long as you are not going to tell me you are pregnant, I couldn't take that and Andy would be in hysterics".

" Don't be so bloody daft, just call me when you can, I have some interesting news".

With that Sara set off towards the lifts and Mags checked her watch to see if it was time to meet Duncan. He had a lot of explaining to do, he had lied to her, he wasn't what he appeared and she felt deeply let down and hurt. The watch was, like the clock on her wall, having a go slow but she decided to go and have coffee anyway, he would turn up later and then it was time for serious talk and a lot of explanation.

Over a cup of coffee she sat and reflected upon what she had learnt. The situation at the antique dealers was becoming quite clear. The old man had been abusing his daughter, amongst others, wife was having an affair, they had moved around a bit too. That moving might suggest that he had been up to his tricks all over the place and now Andy could do some real digging, especially if she can get a proper location for the time in London. The big problem was how much Duncan knew and why he had been so devious in what he had said. Men, she thought, bloody typical, and I thought I had found one that was different.

As thoughts hovered around in her brain, other thoughts interrupted, excuses even, and confusion became deep concern. It was after all natural that he would be reluctant to talk of the experience of his wife as a young child. Yes that was reasonable. He did say he wanted to get revenge for her, but she had insisted that the matter be left alone and he was caring so perhaps he did as she had asked. There was the matter of something he had not told her, his big regret, so it is possible that he did actually do something, but what, surely not murder. It also drifted into her thoughts that she had not actually told him what happened on her final day so it would be amazing if he had been able to make a link with the past. No details had been shared, no names or anything like that so there was no way he could have shared any previous knowledge with her. She so wanted Duncan to be able to show he had nothing to do with it, but doubts and questions jumped about and demanded attention. There was nothing to do but face it straight on, no dodging the issue but a point blank series of questions that insisted on answers. At this moment he private musing came to an abrupt halt.

" Hi Mags, lovely to see you, can I get you another coffee?" Duncan had arrived.

Chapter.28

Once he was seated Mags took a deep breath and announced ,in a serious tone, that they needed to talk.

" That sounds ominous, what on earth is the problem?"

" Well quite simply I have not told you much about something that happened some time ago and there are things connected with it that you have not told me". " There may be a simple explanation but I need to hear it". " It is to do with my last day at work and that death at the antique shop and I am sure you know more about it than you have let on".

"True I do know a bit about it, but it is not what you think, and I did not realise that it was that business that you were involved in." I have not lied to you, but I have not told you all I know." " I just did not make the connection".

" Yes but you almost instantly asked me about murder and manslaughter, which is a bit odd to say the least".

"That was tactless, but a fairly innocent reason for asking such a question". " I had better explain, then you can make up your own mind, walk away and our friendship will probably be over".

Duncan went on in hushed voice to tell Mags what he knew. It was true the Reginald Morris of the antique shop was the same pub landlord that he detested because of what had happened to his beloved Helen. There was little doubt that his daughter, Victoria, suffered the same, but she had never uttered a word about it. Soon after the incident they left the pub on the Vale Estate and went to run one in London. It was years later that they returned to open the antique shop and he, Duncan, had heard that Victoria ran away from home and there had been no trace of her. At that time, some thirty years after the incident, the matter was closed between Duncan and Helen and never spoken about. They simply ignored the fact that he was back in the town and had no intention of visiting his shop or meeting up with him.

Well that was how Helen viewed it, but Duncan for his part found he could not simply let it go. The past was indeed the past , but there appeared to be no justice in the world if something was not done. Reginald Morris needed someone to bring him down and Duncan felt an irresistible compulsion to be the one to do it. So strong was this feeling that, about ten years ago he went into the shop to confront him. He had marched up to the counter, announced who he was, reminded him of what he had done and announced his intention to get justice. He, Duncan, was going to expose him for what he was, friends in the Chamber of Commerce and the Council would shun him and his business would collapse. He intended to try and find Victoria and persuade her to come forward and together they will destroy his name and his character.

At this Reginald Morris clutched his chest, staggered about and eased gently to the floor. It was no heart attack, he couldn't even pretend at that, he was so pathetic. Duncan stepped over the groaning body gave it a look if disgust and walked out of the shop.

" But that was twenty years ago you said?", enquired Mags.

" Yes all of that, you are not going to tell me you think I murdered him, or would it have been manslaughter, just because I left him on the floor convinced it was all play acting?"

" Oh shit, I've made a complete fool of myself, whatever must you think of me?" " It had crossed my mind that you had killed him, but I couldn't really believe the thought". " You confronted him all those years ago but my involvement was only last year, I am an idiot, you must think I am dreadful".

" Well you certainly are different, but you care and that is a special quality". " By the way the eye test was fine and I did not need new glasses so having saved up just in case I have some spare cash to take you out for dinner this evening".

" Oh no, I didn't even ask about the glasses did I ?"

" Look there are too many people around here for much conversation, the place is filling up fast, so l will pick you up at seven and we can go for a meal together". " There is a bit more to tell you, after all I have met Victoria again, I have visited the shop, whilst he was alive, but no I did not murder him, but I would not be apologising if I had". " I can't deny that a large part of me wishes I had, perfect revenge, but Helen would never have forgiven me for dragging it all up and now you know why I just could not tell her, not even on her final day with me".

With that he rose to his feet smiled at Mags and walked towards the door. " I will pick you up a seven so be ready, then we can chat some more and you can tell me what it is that is bugging you".

With a wave of his hand he stepped into the street leaving a stunned Mags sitting looking at the cold remains of her coffee.

Chapter 29

It was early evening and Mags was getting ready for the arrival of Duncan. Sara was not to know but it was not the most helpful time to telephone, but call she did.

" Look", said mags, " I am just getting ready to go out for dinner but I do have a lot to tell you".

" I think I may have found the daughter, and I have discovered a great deal more too". " For a start the brother is not the brother he is the long term boyfriend and now he has a half share in the lot". " He can't be trusted, he has a lot to gain from the death, a simple life for a start and plenty of cash". " I can't tell you much over the phone, Duncan is due here any minute, but I will need to talk to Andy, probably at length when he has a few hours to spare". "It has all got a bit complicated but I am so close to coming up with a lot of answers to questions that have not even been asked yet".

"Wow Mags, that is amazing, he will be delighted to hear what you have found out". It was only yesterday that he was adamant that your original thoughts on the whole thing could well have been right all along". " I will get him to call you when he is free and able to come over and hear all about it". " It had better be when I am free because I am dying to hear all the news"." At least Duncan appears not to be a killer, which must be a great relief".

" Yes, that did have me a bit worried, but he does have a few things to tell me about it and tonight is the night as they say". " If anything staggering comes to light I will let you know straight away, oh he is at the door, speak later"

Duncan stood framed in the doorway and was ushered inside quickly. Mags wanted to apologise for what she had thought and what she had said, but the words did not come out. Instead she moved close to Duncan and gave him a gentle kiss on the cheek. For his part Duncan just smiled at her and laid a comforting arm upon her shoulder.

" Hope you like Italian food, I've booked a table at the place on the London Road out by the bypass roundabout, so we can go whenever you are ready".

"Italian sounds great, that should put a few pounds on then I will have to exercise to shed it all again", Mags laughed.

" You look in good shape to me, madam, your transport awaits"

Chapter 30.

Over the meal Duncan dominated the conversation. Mags sat quieter than she had ever done before and listened intently to what he had to say. He explained that he had no idea that she was the officer who had found the body. He had no idea that she felt sure that there was more to it than an old man collapsing with a heart attack. Yes, she was right there was more to it than that but if she had been open with him at the start then he could have saved her a great deal of trouble. Reginald Morris was a danger to young girls, well at least two, and he, Duncan had the evidence of that. Of course his own daughter ran away as she could no longer take the abuse from him. Somewhere out there was evidence of further abuse, but the man was dead so bringing him to trial was not an option. There was little the police or the courts could do, except try and bring some closure to the victims. Well that was unlikely to help as they already had the closure that they sought. Each had moved on to a life that was untouched by him and for one his death was a closure of its own.

At this point Duncan suggested that they ignore the dessert menu and go straight on to coffee and surprised Mags by his next remark.

" Look I know you have questions you want answers to, so ask and I will give it to you straight, I have nothing to hide". " I wanted the man dead, I may have inadvertently helped that along, but I do not believe I killed him, but I only wish I had". "How do you tell a dying wife that you may have frightened her abuser years ago and planned to go after him again many years later?" " She passed away never knowing that I had confronted him and had every intention of destroying his reputation in any way I could".

" I am so sorry, I sensed there was a background that needed digging out, I almost gave up and let the past be buried with him, but what you told me, Duncan, kick started my thinking". "I have questions but most of the blanks I can fill in for myself". " If you didn't get him then Victoria must have and you clearly know where she can be found".

" I did not say Victoria did anything, in fact I can confirm that he was still very much alive when she last saw him because I was with her".

" Bloody hell" mumbled Mags. " There are some questions I would like answers to but I don't know where to begin".

"Well, if we go back to your place for another drink I can fill in the blanks for you". "You surprise me that you have not mentioned the slimy Gregory, who has now moved in and taken over". " He is a real villain if you want one and she deserves all that she gets". "I cringed when Victoria told me that her mother knew what was going on and did nothing to help or comfort her, some mother she was". " She is now hooked up with a real shady piece of work and if he ruins her then another bit of justice will have taken place".

" How shady is this Gregory chap then Duncan?"

" We can talk about that at your place, but I can probably give your former colleagues a few tips on some of the things he has been up to". " I bet it did not dawn on any of you to check some of the stock, quite a bit of dubious stuff there amongst the usual antiques". " If the old man had known what was happening under his nose, both wife and stock, then he would have blown a fuse". " The sad thing was that he was so past it, he left all the paperwork to his wife, in fact half the time he did not have a clue about anything". " He was just a name over the door, a sucker, a patsy and a dirty old man".

Chapter 31.

When Andy and Sara came to see Mags they were hardly ready for what she had to tell them. Andy sat in stunned silence and as the tale unfolded he began to feel a grin of gigantic proportions spread across his face. He had always admired Mags, she was an irresistible force, and her intuition was the stuff of legends.

Mags calmly told them all that she had found out, but was very careful not to disclose her source of information. Duncan had to be protected, he was innocent of everything, all he was guilty of was loving his wife with very ounce of his being.

As Mags informed them of what she now knew Andy and Sara were simply amazed. Absolutely none of the officers who had dealings in the case had even a clue as to what it was all about. Even the Boss would be astounded.

It was actually very simple, Mags explained. Reginald Morris ran a local pub, had been systematically abusing his daughter, and another girl, or maybe more. The daughter ran away and they moved to another pub in London. Here Mrs.Morris met a man called Gregory, who was a bit of a villain but they began a relationship. Almost certainly the old man knew nothing of this. Years later they moved back to set up the antique shop, but it was pretty certain that the wife did all the business, with the help of Gregory of course, who was always in the background.

In the meantime the husband of the other abused girl confronted Morris and threatened to expose him. Morris pretended to have a heart attack and this man quietly left. No wonder old man Morris withdrew from the Council and all those other public jobs. That was years ago so , although it has a bearing on what happened, it was not anything to do with the final death. Mags went on to explain that this man, who was to be protected at all costs, somehow found the daughter and they agreed to confront him together. They did this on the morning of his death, but once again he gave a poor impression of a heart attack but he was very much alive when they left. They were happy that they had scared him and had seized the opportunity to tell him exactly what they thought of him. They may even have thought that he might be man enough to offer some apology.

" Now listen carefully because one mistake and you blow the whole bloody thing apart", insisted Mags.

"I have a few loose ends to tie up, probably by tomorrow, but you need to get busy right now"

" The man Gregory needs looking into, and the shop stock needs a better check, with a London angle in mind". " I would leave the wife alone for a few days until I can fill in the blanks but there is little doubt that she knows much more than she is letting on". " I have a very good idea of what actually happened but at the moment it is a guess, not fact, but tell the Boss to give me the freedom of a couple of days and he can take it from there"

"Any questions?"

"Mags you are amazing", Andy replied. " That all makes a lot of sense and knowing you the facts can easily be proved".

" Why the hell did you have to retire, we need you to solve all our puzzles and problems"

" I'm too stunned to say anything" said Sara, " I will put the kettle on and make us all another drink".

Andy, over a cup of coffee, promised Mags that he would wait for two days before taking any action but insisted that the Boss needed to be told.

" But what about this Duncan of yours?", enquired Sara.

" Ah well when this is over I shall invite him to stay overnight as he deserves a reward and I intend to make sure he gets one!"

The trio laughed and smiled together as their imaginations ran riot.

Chapter 32

" Duncan, I need to see you so I am coming straight over, no excuse, I will be with you in a few minutes".

When Mags was in a decisive mood she moved mountains, she shattered stumbling blocks and more often than not caused mayhem. That was her style and her friends loved her for it. This was the Mags that was so much respected by her colleagues.

On arrival at Duncan's house she marched in and sat herself down. She explained that she needed a few quick answers and a little help and no was not an option. He would be protected, as he had done nothing wrong, indeed she would have confronted the bastard too, but probably more violently.

Mags told Duncan that she would find it helpful to talk to Victoria if he could arrange it, but she was to be assured that she was not in any trouble. A difficult thing to ask but it was important. All Mags needed was confirmation from Duncan that when he and Victoria left the shop the old man was alive, preferably with a little detail of what he was doing other than pretending once again to have the attack. Position on the floor, was anything broken, all that kind of stuff. The final part of the jigsaw was the question of anyone else being there or at least close at hand, like the wife or the man Gregory.

Duncan paused then began to fill in the final blanks.

" Well the shop had only just opened when we went in".

"He was putting some bits of stuff in a glass cabinet".

"We walked up to him and he did not even recognise his own daughter".

" I reminded him who I was and that I told him years ago that I would destroy him for what he had done"

" He looked quite shocked when I told him Helen was now dead so I had nothing holding me back as she could not suffer any more pain".

" Victoria told him who she was and he looked even more shocked".

"Together we told him that justice was now to be done and the whole world was to find out what he had done"

"At this he staggered to his swivel chair and slumped into it".

" The heart attack trick came on again, but you could tell it was an act because he kept staring at Victoria and swearing at us".

" We did not see anyone else around, turned to leave, believing we had done what we went to do, and he called out "sod you" as we left and walked off into the street".

" I shook hands with Victoria and we went our separate ways, although we have kept in touch and I see her now and again with her family".

" Yes, her family, she is a grandmother now, so she too managed to get the past well behind her and create a life for herself, and I won't let anyone muck that up for her".

Mags, not for the first time, moved over to Duncan and kissed him. It was a kiss of love, a kiss of relief and a kiss that told him how much she cared.

" Do you think you could get away with one last visit to that shop, Duncan, I have an idea and want to try it out?"

" What the hell are you planning?"

Mags went on to explain that she had already visited the shop and got a lot of information from the cleaner. She wanted to tease out a tiny bit more information if possible, even meet Mrs.Morris, as they had never met before. If Duncan was sure that she would not recognise him, then they could go as partners, as she had told the cleaner, buy a pendant and let her intuition have free reign.

Duncan agreed that he could see no problem, he had not see Mrs.Morris since he was a teenager, so no chance of her recognising her. He seemed quite keen on the idea of playing detective, even if he was under orders to say nothing other than yes dear and pay up when asked.

" When are we going to do this Mags".

"Now, get your coat on, you can drive".

When they entered the shop the cleaner was standing by the counter and recognised Mags instantly.

" Hello come back to get the pendant have you".

"Yes, I got tied up the last time and could not back to see you before you closed".

The cleaner produced the pendant from the display and laid it out on the counter. Duncan looked at it and wondered who on earth would pay £20 for a thing like that, then realised that he was about to do just that.

" All alone today again?" ,asked Mags.

" Oh no, Mrs.Morris is here".

At this point an elderly lady appeared from behind the curtain at the back of the shop and beside her was a man, much younger, slightly scruffy and in a crumpled suit.

" I am the owner of the shop, I was just doing a little paperwork in the office here at the back". " "That is where I am usually found as I have staff now to deal with customers as I can't rush about as swiftly as I once did".

The scruffy man in the suit smiled a kind of smile, although to Mags it appeared to be more of a smirk.

" Well my partner has agreed to buy me the pendant so all he has to do is pay up".

Duncan reached for his wallet, handed over the cash and with the pendant neatly boxed and in a little bag, they made their way to the door and left.

" Thought you were going to probe questions and get answers".

" Oh I did Duncan, oh I certainly did, I now know all I need to know".

" Detective work is about using your brain to save your feet, it is about being to add up without using a calculator". " We have done brilliantly and I can now see how this whole thing can be wrapped up without you or Victoria being involved, although you may have to talk privately to a very dear friend of mine, but that can be done at my house". " You were a star, Duncan, an enormous help, even if you only did as I asked and said nothing".

"When you are around I can't get a ruddy word in edgeways anyway!"

Andy could hardly contain his delight when Mags told him all that she now knew. The way forward was clear and surprisingly easy. He had already got people working on notes of the stock at the shop and they had already found links to robberies all around the London area. Gregory was the key, so a further visit to the shop was planned so that they could nail him properly. There was already enough to question him and a lot of pushing might just save everyone a lot of work. The link to the death of Mr. Morris was a little more difficult, but the Boss had said he would handle the interview himself and intended to be forceful, but within the law.

This was where Mags bowed out gracefully, but the promise stood that she would be kept fully informed. If her guess was right they might add manslaughter to the charges as well. That would give Gregory something to think about.

Mags rang Duncan to tell him the news and that at long last it was all over. He, Duncan, had kept the promise he made to himself, his beloved Helen could rest in peace and old man Morris got what he deserved anyway whoever caused his death.

Two days later as Mags was dusting and tidying a car that she knew well pulled into her drive. She rushed to the door to greet the Boss , who had Andy with him.

" Got news already?"

" Yes all done, the Boss was brilliant, he had him telling us everything in a matter of minutes".

" Steady Andy, you don't have to flatter me to get the promotion you deserve".

" Look Mags, how long would it take to get this chap of yours over here, it would be nice to fill in all the blanks together as I understand he was your inspirational key".

" I'll ring him now, hopefully he can be here in ten minutes".

They sat and drank coffee until Duncan arrived and introductions were made.

" Look Duncan, I wanted, as a courtesy, to have you here to get the full facts of what happened".

"It became very easy once I had a real go at Gregory in interview, even the duty solicitor sat quiet and open-mouthed".

" Well he was brought in about a range of stolen goods found in the shop". " He soon owned up that he was involved in finding suitable targets and then a group of friends took the valuable items for him to pass on through the shop".

" That bit was easy, but he went into a sweating panic when I told him that I was also considering charging him with the murder of Reginald Morris". " He did not need much of a push from me and he was telling everything".

" When you, Duncan, and his daughter confronted him in the shop that morning, Gregory and Mrs.Morris were in their usual place behind the curtain. Once you left they came out and screamed and yelled at him". " Mrs Morris, told him with great delight that she had known about his abuse but she did not care because she had a young lover who did more for than he ever did". " Gregory told him that his precious business was a sham and how some stock actually got there". " As they tormented him he fell to the floor, knocking over a vase he had been cleaning and had a heart attack" " Mrs. Morris stood and watched him, announced that they should let him die and when they were sure he had breathed his last, went out the back, got into the car and went shopping".

" So Mags, thanks to you, several other forces, are praising us for helping solve a whole fist full of crimes, but we also have two people in custody charged with at least manslaughter".

" I am thrilled, but thanks go to Duncan too, but to tell you the truth I had already decided that the old man got what he deserved and if the guilty party had been anyone I care about I would have kept my mouth firmly shut".

" Anyway I shall show Duncan how much I care later tonight when you lot have all gone".

" Oh by the way, Mags, on that sort of subject, I need to tell you that Sara is expecting, she will be calling you later".

" You careless bugger, I knew I should have insisted you have those bloody condoms!"

About the Author

Stuart Bell had been an headteacher of Primary Schools, before his retirement. He spent forty years weaving stories for children and has now turned his attention to a maturer reader, many of whom may well be former pupils who recall some of the stories that he told. During his many years in education, he was Deputy Chief Marker for English and was co-author of a series of six books, "Success in English" to guide pupils and their parents, and to provide practice. He spent the later years of his working life, and a few years of retirement, as an educational consultant.

After a few years as a widower he has returned to writing thanks to the support and encouragement of family and close friends. He had always said that he would write a novel for the adult world and with the special support of the people dearest to him he has now fullfilled that promise.

Stuart lives in Mid-Kent, near where he ended his educational career. He has his family quite near to him and is very much a father and proud grandfather. He maintains close contact with a number of former colleagues and one particular special friend who has encouraged him to use his love of language to create stories to intrigue, amuse and entertain.